Durell listened, waiting for special sounds. Sounds of silence. Sounds of death.

Durell had killed before; he was an expert at it. He could destroy a man in many ways, using his hands, his feet, a roll of paper, a needle, a knife. It was a necessary part of his business. He had seen men die, men who had been his friends, but who allowed one fatal moment of distraction to overcome them. It was a strange war he engaged in, lonely and dark, and he knew he was no longer like most other men. His long years with K Section had changed him in ways he did not like, but which were necessary for survival. Survival was the name of the game.

Now he could smell danger. This time it was close. Very close.

Fawcett Gold Medal Books
by Edward S. Aarons:

EDWARD S. AARONS

Assignment Afghan Dragon

FAWCETT GOLD MEDAL • NEW YORK

ASSIGNMENT AFGHAN DRAGON

© 1976 CBS Publications, The Consumer Publishing Division of CBS Inc.

ISBN: 0-449-14085-7

Printed in the United States of America

2   3   4   5   6   7   8   9   10   11

For Kathy

In the beginning, P'an Ku, the giant, labored for eighteen thousand years to construct the world with his hammer and chisel. He dug out the seas, and built the mountains, the valleys and the rivers. His companion was the Dragon.

The Dragon is the greatest of all beasts, the one most filled with the principles of Yang. He is larger than large, smaller than small, stronger than strong, wider than wide. His breath is a cloud upon which he flies up to Heaven in the spring. In the autumn, he sleeps at the bottom of the sea. He rides the skies, visible or invisible. He possesses a pearl which is the soul of the moon. He is everywhere and nowhere; no man can find him.

—Chinese Legend

1

Desolation lay all around him.

He stood quietly in the hot wind out of the Dasht-i-Lut and heard the harsh whisper of sand slithering across the outcrop of reddish rock. He tried to listen with all his senses. Overhead, the sun struck at him out of a coppery, oppressive sky, unrelenting and implacable, a weight upon his head and shoulders like the pressure of an unforgiven sin. A single vulture began to circle high in the glaring heavens, patient and filled with deadly grace. In a moment, it was joined by a companion, and the next time he looked, through the sheltering lenses of his sunglasses, there were three. Sweat trickled from the nape of his neck and down his spine, collecting on his shoulder blades, soaking his khaki shirt, spilling in endless rivulets across his belly and down his groin and legs. The gun in his right hand felt like a child's toy against the infinite hostility of the elements.

Durrell felt lost, but he was not lost; he felt alone, but he knew he was not alone.

Behind him, where he had left the corrugated dirt road—a graveled thread coursing pitifully across the rocky landscape—a low ridge of reddish rock, which was carved grotesquely by eons of wind, hid the top of his Toyota Land Cruiser. He had rented it in Kerman, after

Jules Eaton had been refused a landing permit in Zahidan. Air traffic was temporarily bogged down in red tape. There was little traffic in this direction. He listened to the singing silence of the wind. Tongues of sand, pushed by elemental forces, wriggled against his boots. A telephone pole canted above the top of the little ridge beside the road. In the distance were the purple mountains of the Mokran, where the black-robed Baluchi tribesmen lived. He heard something bang, thump and creak. And again. Bang, thump, creak. Artifact. Man-made. But out of sight along the rutted track that led downward and to the left and vaguely north, beyond another outcrop of rock.

Most of the day he had been driving through this emptiness, trapped between the coastal mountains along the Gulf of Oman and the carved sands of the Dasht-i-Lut. The hot smells of sand and rock, the malodorous whiff of an occasional camel train passed with care along the track, the reek of a diesel oil truck now and then, had filled his nostrils and every pore of his body. Now he smelled something strange—methane, marsh gas, sulphurous and noxious. He was near the briny waters of the outer Hamun Lakes, more particularly, Lake Hab. He wished Fingal had chosen another rendezvous. It would have been easier to let Jules Eaton fly him on to Meshed, to contact Fingal in the relative comforts of that Shi'ite town dedicated to Islam's God with its fairy-tale palaces and minarets, its mosques and tombs dedicated to ancient greatness. But Fingal had insisted that they meet here, and Durell's briefing was fixed and obdurate.

Search and deliver, he thought.

Bang. Creak. Thump.

Durell moved at last, having waited five minutes after turning off the Toyota's engine to let its sound die away, fading, beating, echoing. He walked forward. His boots grated on sharp shards of stone that twinkled and refracted the white light of the sky. The track led downward another two hundred feet, and he smelled the swamp gas again, carried on the hot, scouring wind. It made him think briefly of the Louisiana bayous, of dark rich delta land, trails through the live oaks and narrow dikes that afforded footing inches above the muddy, stagnant water. His boyhood was long ago and far away. The world had changed, losing its simple naivety; slogans were despised, patriotism scorned; suspicion and cynicism were today's watchwords. And all the while a thermonuclear weight hung just below the horizon, like a devastating offspring of the sun that beat down on him at this moment. It was a weight delicately and precariously balanced only by the efforts of many men like Durell, against lust and madness and the inexcusability of potential error.

He looked at his watch. He was fifteen minutes late for his rendezvous with Fingal. A trailer-tank had jackknifed on the road through the Mokran mountains to the south, sliding into a Baluchi camel caravan, killing two nameless nomads and four proud, robed women in the ensuing explosion. He had been worried about the police then, who were cold and efficient, regarding him as a foreigner, a *ferenghi*. His cover papers that described him as an American archaeologist on his way to join Professor Berghetti's Italian expedition had sufficed. They hadn't found his weapons. But the delay made him this late, and he began to regret it and worry about it. You could plan and lay out a seemingly faultless operation, and an accident, unforeseen and destructive, could throw the whole thing, crumpled and useless, into the wastebasket.

He paused. *Bang. Thump.*

He turned a corner of the trail and saw the little enclave of stone huts clustered around a long-dry well, with its dead date palms, and some old nomad's private domain, abandoned in endless time, perhaps only last year, perhaps a century ago. Except for the pressures of wind and sand, there was little to change the shape of things here.

"Fingal?" he called softly.

No one answered. Nothing lived here except the three —no, four, now—vultures circling the copper sky with hungry patience. Durell paused for another long minute and considered the angular shadows cast by the tumbledown huts. The sun would set in two hours, he guessed. He sniffed at the methane gas from the swamps, still some miles away to the north and east, according to his maps.

There was one main house amid the date palm stumps where the roof had fallen in. The north wall had collapsed in a rubble of dried mud bricks that perhaps had been built in the same tradition as those of ancient Mesopotamia. Aside from the dilapidated wreckage of some machinery, scavenged beyond identity, he could have been back in pre-Biblical days. He felt oddly reluctant to proceed. The gun in his hand, which should have felt reassuring, was simply hot and heavy, perhaps impotent.

Durell was a tall man, with thick black hair touched with gray at the temples. He had a heavy musculature, that was deceiving, since he moved with a light grace and a deft precision; his hands were long-fingered, the hands of a gambler adept at cards, perhaps inherited from his old Grandpa Jonathan, who had been one of the last of the Mississippi riverboat gamblers. He was a far distance from that time and place. He had been in this business a long time, he thought; perhaps too long. He was not a stranger to danger. The rhythm of the words made his mouth quirk. Behind the metal-rimmed sunglasses, his eyes were a very dark blue, almost black when he was thoughtful or angered. There was a time when he had indulged himself in a moustache, but it had become an identifying mark, listed in too many dossiers, and he had shaved it off long ago.

"Fingal?" he called again.

Homer Fingal had always been a fool, a dominated man, a man he would not have chosen for this rendezvous. A bit pompous about his rebellion from an authoritative family and breeding. His father's name was Wellington, but Fingal had married a girl named Sarah Fingal, and as a gesture to demonstrate his "now" presence and his acceptance of equality between the sexes, and perhaps to defy and irritate his father, he had taken Sarah's maiden name for his own. He had been rejected for the Foreign Service, of course, and several posts in State. McFee, the boss of K Section, had picked him up mainly because Homer Fingal was a top-rated Orientalist.

Durell moved on down into the deserted settlement.

His boots grated on the sharp shale of the descent. The wind shifted again, and he felt a surprisingly fresh drift of air from the cooler blue lakes to the north. A sand-devil whipped and whirled around the caved-in well for a moment. The first hut was empty. The second held the skeleton of a dog, dusty and dry, webbed with filaments of unidentifiable stuff. Little mounds of discarded debris, half covered with sand, lay here and there in the compound. But the tracks of Fingal's vehicle, wide tires designed for sand and shale, led in an arc turning behind the central house. Durell paused. The sun seared the back of his neck. Sweat fogged his sunglasses. The wind died.

Finally, taking his time, cautious in the manner that defied K Section's computer analysis of his survival factor, he turned the corner and found Homer Fingal, almost as he had expected.

It was a place for death, but not this kind of death.

The long, thin body had been staked out with pegs between the stumps of two dead date palms. Fingal was naked, and there was no sign of his clothes. Durell did not approach closer than ten feet, studying the crude camel's hair ropes that stretched from wrist and ankle to the wooden pegs driven into the sand; then he considered the scuffed footprints all around. He thought of booby traps, of explosives hidden in some innocent-looking item just lying about. He saw Fingal's car, a dusty, hard-driven Chevrolet that must have cost a small fortune to bring into Iran. Or perhaps it had come with one of K Section's shipments. Funds were no problem on this job. The assignment had Q clearance. Durell walked carefully to the battered sedan, put his hands on the open driver's window, quickly withdrew them when the heat seared his palms. Fingal's jacket lay across the back of the driver's seat, behind the wheel. He did not touch it. When he looked back at the body staked between the palm stumps, he saw the thin chest lift uncertainly in a shallow breath.

He turned and walked slowly back and smelled the

man. It wasn't just that Fingal was dead, although his body did not know it yet. They—he was sure it had been more than one man who had trapped Fingal here—had done a fine, savage job on him. Flies buzzed around the thick clots of blood in the crotch, where Fingal's genitals had been hacked off. Even worse, they had surgically, most precisely, excised Fingal's eyelids, so that the eyes were open and blind, the eyeballs curiously wrinkled from dehydration as they stared up into the glare of the sun. Fingal's thin, sandy-colored beard, one that he usually cropped meticulously, stood straight up, stiff as a shaving brush. The man's mouth was open, and Durell could see the gold fillings in his teeth when he brushed away the buzz of flies.

He knelt beside the body.

"Fingal?"

The chest heaved convulsively, and he could see the failing heart beat under the ribs.

"Fingal?"

The lips moved, quaking, closing, opening, like an old man without teeth.

"Yo." The whispered sound was softer than that of the sound driven by the wind.

"It's Sam. Sam Durell."

"You—you're too late."

"It couldn't be helped. Fingal—?"

"Kill me, Sam."

Durell unscrewed the cap on the water canteen hooked to his belt under his bush jacket. He carefully dribbled a few drops on the parched, cracked, white lips.

"Kill me now. Please."

"Take it easy."

Even while he knelt, his attention concentrated on the whispering sounds that came from Fingal's mouth, he was aware of the sand blowing, the dead palm stumps, the smell of brine and the smell of Fingal's body, and of the vultures circling in the high yellow vault of the sky.

Durell said, "You've been here for hours. I'm only fifteen minutes late. Can you tell me what happened?"

"Dawn," whispered the white mouth. "All day. I'm glad it's night now."

Fingal was blind.

Durell said, "Who did it?"

"Hmmmm-mmmm."

Durell dribbled more water between the teeth. The man's beard had been waxed, and the wax had melted in the heat, but it still stood erect, somehow obscene. Some of the skin had been removed in careful patches from Fingal's belly and flanks. Some of his toes had been chopped off, and both thumbs. The mortal wound was difficult to see. Probably in the back. Fingal was glued to the sand with his dried, crusted blood.

"It wasn't supposed to be like this," Durell said. "No violence. You were detailed only to take me to where Nuri Qam is hiding. He's the one who borrowed me from K Section, right? Mr. Qam asked for me. A matter of diplomatic courtesy. You were just a messenger, Fingal. What did they want from you?"

"The dragon," Fingal whispered.

"What dragon?" Durell thought Fingal might be hallucinating in his last moments before dying. "Do you mean Berghetti's dragon?"

"Yo."

"They asked you about it?"

"Yuh. Sam?"

"All right, Fingal."

"I hurt. Kill me. Did you see what they did?"

"I'll get you out of here," Durell said.

"No, no! Don't move me."

From far away, Durell heard the sound of a truck rumbling along the rough highway where he had left the Toyota.

"Go to Meshed," Fingal whispered. "Nuri Qam came across the border there from Afghanistan."

"Meshed? I thought he'd be in Kabul."

"He's there. Sam?"

"No, I won't do it, Fingal."

"Please."

"No. Tell me—"

"Say goodbye to Sarah. Don't—tell her—what they did."

All at once, without warning, Fingal was dead.

2

Durell took the keys from the Chevrolet. He would have liked to splash the vehicle with gasoline and toss a match on it, but the fire and smoke would inevitably bring police, even to this barren place, and he did not want that. He did not linger in his thoughts about the way Fingal had died. In Durell's business, you went as silently and as unobtrusively as possible, in life as well as in death. Fingal had not been trained for its darkness and cunning, and although Durell had never been close to the man, he felt anger at the way Fingal had been used and betrayed. He had no doubt that there was betrayal here, because Fingal had been led to believe the mission was a simple one, merely that of a courier to relay a single scrap of information in a puzzle whose outlines Durell could scarcely perceive as yet. He wondered briefly what Fingal's father, General Wellington, would think when he learned of Fingal's death. The old man, the terror of the Pentagon and close ear to Sugar Cube, might only be relieved that his embarrassing, scholarly son was finally out of the way. He did not think Fingal's wife, Sarah, would feel quite the same way.

He took his time destroying the identity of the Chevrolet as much as possible; he removed the license plates and buried them in the sand at some distance, smoothing the sand into wind ripples to conceal the cache. He could do nothing about the serial numbers on the engine. On the back seat he found two books, slim volumes that were well-dog-eared and annotated: the first was a collection of classical, monochrome, black-and-white paintings ranging from the tenth to the eighteenth centuries, with quite adequate reproductions of Mu Ch'i's tiger and Lo Chih-Ch'uan's delicate landscapes. One page had been turned down over an illustration of a thirteenth-century print of Ma Lin's, a misty storm of black ink. The text was in Chinese, and the word *ch'i-yün,* spirit resonance, had been underlined.

It didn't seem to mean anything.

The second book was a thin volume of Taoist poetry and interpretation, also in Chinese, by the Chinese scholar Ch'u Ta-kao. Durell opened the yellowed leaves at random. *Tao produces all things. Virtue feeds them. All things appear in different forms and each is perfected by its innate power.*

Durell put both books in his bush jacket pocket and turned away to climb the hill back to the highway.

The sun was lower now, but the impact of its heat struck as forcefully as before. The wind had died completely. Durell moved faster now, not looking back at Fingal's body. In a few moments, the abandoned oasis was out of sight and below him. Sweat stained his back. He started to put his gun away, tucking it into his belt, and then he saw the roof of his Toyota and saw that another vehicle was parked behind it, and he remembered the rumbling sound of a passing car or truck on the rough, graveled road while he was down below. The vehicle had not passed. He stopped short and listened and presently heard voices, a male, another male, and then a female giggled. It sounded harmless enough. Even reassuring. He swung right, keeping below the rim of the road embankment, and when he had gone about fifty yards, he climbed again and came out on the road behind the two cars parked there.

The second vehicle was a VW van, ancient, rusty and

dusty to the point where the original painting, all sworls and blobs, was barely visible under the coating of desert sand. The license plate was Afghani. This place was, after all, only about forty miles from the Afghan-Iranian border.

The two young men and the girl seemed unarmed and harmless enough, and he did not think they were aware of his presence behind them, as they explored his Toyota, climbing in and out with a youthful, animallike curiosity punctuated by the girl's laughter and the men's comments. He was being ripped off. They had removed his extra jerry cans, his spare water tank, his battered leather luggage. They were speaking to each other in English— American accent—and apparently enjoying themselves. One was smoking a cigarette, but he could not smell the smoke from here and couldn't be sure if it was pot or just plain tobacco.

"Hey!"

The fat one had turned, lugging the plastic water can, and saw him standing there, a tall, enigmatic silhouette against the lowering sun.

"Hey, people," the fat one said.

They all turned to stare at him, guilt and some surprise on their faces, changing in a swift blur to defiance and animosity, even resentment, that their thieving game was about to be interrupted.

"Hey, Charley."

The taller one, thin and dark-haired, with a strange intensity that could be dangerous, hooked his thumbs in his wide, brass-studded belt. They were all bare-footed, dirty, unkempt in blue jeans, tie-dyed, and shirts of ancient stripes that hadn't seen wash-water for some time. The girl, also dark-haired, slim and somehow of better quality than the two men, tossed back her long black hair. She grinned slowly. The fat one looked worried, holding the water can. The thin one happened to be empty-handed, and Durell watched his dirty toes curl slowly and tensely into the dust of the road.

"So there he is," the girl said. Her voice hinted at distant cultivation. "No more fun and games. My, he looks

angry. Mister, we just found your car and figured it was
broken down and you went off somewhere on a lift."

"Nature called," Durell said.

"My, aren't we delicate; ha-ha, you had to take a crap,
you mean?"

Durell kept his eyes on the tall, dark one with the
angry, intense eyes, who said, "Shut up, Annie . . . You
American?"

"Yes."

"We were borrowing some of your stuff. Finder's
keepers, we figured."

"Put it back," Durell said.

"Sure."

"All of it."

"Sure."

"Now."

"My, my," the girl named Annie said. "Isn't he the
hard-nosed establishment type, Charley."

Charley was the dark man with the curled toes. The fat
boy turned and tossed the water can back into the rear
seat of the Toyota. The can was heavy, but he made the
gesture without effort; he was stronger and harder than he
looked. The girl shrugged and swung Durell's luggage into
the back seat, too. The man named Charley kept staring,
motionless, at Durell.

"What's down there?"

"Nothing," Durell said.

"There are some old tracks."

"They go to a dry well. Some abandoned houses.
What's your last name, Charley?" Durell asked.

"Anderson."

"Are you going to start something?"

The man's eyes touched the gun in Durell's belt. His
teeth gleamed in a vague smile. His eyes were hard and
reluctant. "I guess not."

"Good."

It was not uncommon to spot American youths in this
desolate part of the world. Marijuana, hash and heroin
were cheap and easily available. Some of them had gone
into petty smuggling; they became minor entrepreneurs,

supplying the big drug syndicates; they survived that way. Others often gravitated to the larger towns like Kabul, and gave blood donations to gain the money needed to support their habits, if they were too far gone to be enterprising on their own. This trio, with their van, looked relatively affluent, despite their outward grubbiness. Durell would not have been surprised to learn that their college degrees came from prestigious Ivy League universities.

The girl, Annie, said, "Oh, hell, let's get going, Charley."

Charley was the obvious leader. He said nothing. His fat young friend stepped on his cigarette and began picking at his nose, engrossed in what he found there. The girl moved toward Durell with a defiant swagger, a swing of ample hips, a jiggle of her breasts under the shirt that made it plain she disdained a bra.

"And what's your name, stranger?" she asked, mocking a Western accent.

"Durell," he said.

"I'm Annie Jackson. You know Charley Anderson. Mortimer—Mort Jones here—is tripping a bit. You don't mind?"

"It's your business," Durell said.

"We've been here a couple of months. It's a real trip. Where are you headed for? You with one of the oil companies?"

"Ur-Kandar," Durell said.

"That's the next village, huh?"

"Yes. And you?"

"We, too."

Their car was headed in the wrong direction, but Durell said nothing about it. He watched Mort and Annie reload his Toyota. Charley's toes slowly uncurled in the dust of the road. Finally he bobbed his head, as if he had made a decision, having absorbed all of Durell with his intense, angry eyes, and then he joined his companions.

Nothing more was said. Hostility lingered in the air, wavering like the heat waves over the barren landscape. Durell saw that Anderson had spotted the vultures high in the sky, but perhaps that didn't mean anything to him. In a few minutes, Durell's possessions had been reluctantly returned to his vehicle.

As he swung into the Toyota behind the driver's wheel, he heard the girl calling to him. He switched on the ignition, but then he felt an urgent thump as Annie's hand slapped the side of the car, and he paused. She was not alone. Charley Anderson stood a few steps behind her, his thick black brows twisted into a glowering scowl. The girl held something out to Durell.

"Please. I'd like to apologize."

"What is it?"

"Take it. A peace offering," she said, smiling.

"That's not necessary."

"Please."

Close up, her features were clean and regular, and if she were less unkempt and tidied up, she might even have been beautiful. Her long dark hair was thick and lustrous, even through the desert dust; her mouth was perhaps a bit too wide, but the lower lip was full and generous. Her eyes were gray, dancing with amusement above fine, rather high cheekbones. Her body was lithe, perhaps a bit too thin—was she hungry?—but she had long, sturdy legs, seen through the tight jeans, and equally sturdy hips and thighs.

He saw that what she offered him were two small plastic packets containing a smidgin of white powder in each. Her smile coaxed him.

"Maybe you'd enjoy it," Annie said.

"Do you like being a pusher?" he asked.

"Oh, no. It's nothing like that. This is just by way of apology. And we've got plenty."

Charley Anderson said, "Come on, Annie. He's too straight."

"Well, I don't want him angry at us. He's a fellow American, after all."

"I'm not angry," Durell said.

He thought the urgency in the girl's gray eyes was more than the situation called for, but he couldn't fathom the expression there, and after a moment of staring at her, he put the Toyota into gear and drove away, leaving them and the multicolored van lost in a cloud of dust behind him.

3

Ur-Kandar was a small village beside a tributary lake to Lake Hamun, with one or two modern houses of concrete block and tin roofs, and the rest of mud walls, clusters of Asian compounds along the marsh, briny shore. It was clear that the new dams on the Afghan side of the border, along the Helmand and Khash Rivers, were playing havoc with the water levels here in Iran. The main industry was the weaving of *assirs,* reed window shades, and round boats also made of reeds. The mountains of the Mokran, southward in Baluchistan, loomed with bristling peaks against the horizon. The area was a wide, interconnected series of lakes and ponds and marshlands, trapped between the sands of the Dasht-i-Lut and the mountains. Durell assumed that the far side of the lake, which looked deceptively inviting in the afterglow of the setting sun, was Afghanistan. There were telephone and power lines in Ur-Kandar, and he saw that there was a central post office and Phone Central near the *assir* factory. The Phone Central was marked with the dusty, flaking royal emblem of Iran. A metal Coca-Cola sign hung beside the emblem, marked with Farsi script.

He saw no other cars along the dusty, twisting street where the houses presented their backs to the public, behind high compound walls. At the far end, where the lake shore began, a single ruined Greek column thrust against the purpling sky, and Durell wondered if any of Alexander's armies had marched through this place long, long ago.

The smell of food cooked over charcoal fires pervaded the air, and he realized he was hungry. The police station stood next to the central telephone office, opposite a small faience-decorated mosque, and beyond that was a caravanserai, and old inn with a central courtyard and rickety wooden balconies overlooking the dirt square where several camels and sheep from a Baluchi caravan were already bedded down for the night. The Baluchi, tall proud men in black robes and black tents, watched their stately women preparing their meals over charcoal and camel dung fires. A melodic chanting in deep masculine voices came from somewhere along the lake shore, where several reed fishing boats were drawn up with masts canted against the darkening sky. Just next to the old Greek column, whose majesty still defied more than twenty centuries, was the serpentine minaret above the local mosque.

"Sir? I think very much the accommodations may not be satisfactory—"

The clerk's voice came in Farsi. Durell answered in kind, aware that he had grown a bit rusty in its use since his last visit to Tehran.

"A single room, please."

"Luckily, we are not crowded; the Baluchi use their own tents, but there are few amenities for *ferenghi*. And the room will cost one hundred rials—"

"That's too much. I'm not a stranger here."

"No, you speak our language quite well. We can arrange it, perhaps, since the true proprietor is away in Hormak on family business, may it be successful, Allah willing."

The clerk's desk was simply two boards placed across two rusty oil drums. An old oil lantern, of the type once used on railways, provided the only light in the tiny cubicle that faced the entrance to the inner courtyard. Smoke drifted in from the nomad cooking-fires.

"My name is Chadraqi," said the clerk. "I would suggest you place your car behind the inn. There is a little fencing there, and a shed. Lock it up well and remove what you consider valuable, sir. The boys in Ur-Kandar are thievish. They are only playful, but it might prove annoying."

Durell envisioned the Toyota stripped of wheels and everything moveable. He slid an extra fifty-rial note across the rough counter.

"Let me hire a man to guard it, then."

"Yes, sir." Mr. Chadraqi was pleased. "You are generous. I can get a most reliable man, my brother-in-law, in fact, who can be trusted to remain awake all night—"

"See that he does. And one more thing."

The clerk was expectant, balancing on tip-toes. "Yes, sir?"

"I will need the telephone."

"Ah, sir, that is only open and available for two hours each day, except Friday, from ten o'clock in the morning until the noon prayers."

"Who is in charge of the office?"

"I am, sir."

Durell smiled. "And of course, you can open it for me?"

"That would be against government regulations, I am afraid."

"Rules are meant to be bent, if not broken." He put another note on the plank table. He knew he was being robbed, but the thought of Fingal, and visions of his lidless blind eyes staring into the sun, troubled him even more than before, and he felt impatient.

The deal was quickly made. In an hour, the clerk would be free. He offered to send up dinner, a stew of mutton and eggplant called *khoreshe bandijan,* prepared by his wife, which Durell accepted, along with a pot of thick, hot tea. His room had a small water faucet, of which Mr. Chadraqi was inordinately proud, and Durell could wash there, he said.

The room was a whitewashed cubicle with a metal cot, straw mattress, a rug that might have been colorful once, but now showed only the gray of age. A flimsy door opened onto the wooden gallery, whose rail was burnished by countless greasy hands through the years. The air felt cooler when Durell stepped outside. Night had come. The smell of methane was sharp and discouraging. Overhead, the stars reeled, and he saw in them the glare of Fingal's blind eyes, sliced open to the sun. He looked down at the small cooking fires of the caravan men, who huddled over their food and muttered together in an incomprehensible Mokran dialect, humped shadows that seemed primordial in aspect. He turned back into the room and closed the wooden door to the gallery, lighted a kerosene lamp and searched the cubicle thoroughly, although he expected to find nothing alarming inside.

Later, he stripped off his clothes and washed at the single basin. The faucet issued a single trickle of yellowish, pungent water. He managed to get off most of the desert dust, and then took his Smith & Wesson .38, the heavy metal somehow comforting now, and broke the gun down, wiping and oiling it and carefully checking each cartridge before he reloaded. He listened to the noises in the inn, but heard nothing exceptional.

Durell had killed before; he was an expert at it. He could destroy a man in many ways, using his hands, his feet, a roll of paper, a needle, a knife. It was sometimes a necessary part of his business. He had seen men die, men who had been his friends, but who allowed one fatal moment of distraction to overcome them. It was a strange, silent war he engaged in, lonely and dark, and he knew he was no longer like most other men. His long years with K Section had changed him in ways he did not like, but which were necessary for survival. Survival was the name of the game. He could smell danger from far off, sense it with an instinct derived from training and experience. In a world where information and data from the other side could spell the difference between peace and holocaust, where facts were commodities commanding the highest price, life or death, he had managed to survive reasonably well so far.

When he considered the scars on his body as he bathed

at the washbasin, he recalled the jungles and deserts, the alleys of the world's great cities, its most remote areas. He could sense danger here. He could not as yet put his finger on the source. Fingal, that blunderer, had been killed in a manner which indicated a casual murder and robbery, and his murderers used local methods of cruel amusement to make it look like a chance encounter with strangers. Durell did not believe it. Every stitch of the man's clothing had been taken, but the car had been left behind, and this surely was a prize, if only for its cannibalized parts.

He considered the two thin volumes of Chinese orientalism he had retrieved, and studied each page swiftly, starting with the book of ink sketches, pausing to reread an underlined passage describing the *wen-jen,* the gentlemen-scholars of Chinese ancient centuries. Ink and brush were used both to represent an object, such as a plum tree, and to allude to the plum tree as a reference. The *wen-jen* masters became what they painted, it was believed; the *ch'i,* or spirit of the subject, became part of the artist's hand and then of the ink. Durell closed the book, wondering about Fingal.

In the text of Tao Tê Ching, he read two or three passages, underlined by Fingal:

> *Tao is always inactive*
> *Yet Tao does everything.*
>
> *Kings are increased by being lessened.*
> *It is not desirable to be as prominent*
>   *as a single jewel,*
> *Or as monotonous as a number of*
>   *precious stones.*

None of it seemed to mean very much here in Ur-Kandar.

In an hour he was on the telephone at the government station, led there by Mr. Chadraqi and allowed in through the back door. The place was closed and padlocked, but the clerk had a key to the rear entrance. It smelled of Turkish Tobacco and stale cooking and sweat.

"I will wait outside, sir." Chadraqi seemed a bit nervous. "You will not be long?"

"No longer than necessary," Durell said. As the clerk sidled away, Durell added, "Tell me, have you had many foreigners coming through Ur-Kandar lately?"

"Yes, many, sir. Oil men, travelers of all sorts."

"Any Chinese?"

The clerk looked blank. "Chinese?"

"Diplomats, salesmen, engineers—"

"No, sir."

"None at all?"

"I have never seen a Chinese," said the clerk.

"All right."

"Why do you ask about Chinese?"

"I don't know," Durell said.

When he was alone, he began the tedious work of getting a connection through to Tehran. The instrument clicked, whined, buzzed. The operator sounded as if he were on the moon. He spoke pure Farsi, clearly and distinctly. "Tehran, yes, sir." Then the line went dead. Durell waited. He tried to control his anger. Then, as if the operator had moved himself next door, Durell heard, "The number again, sir?" Durell gave him the number of the U.S. Embassy on Takhte Jamshid Avenue. Another long wait. He looked through the dusty window to the end of the road, where the Greek column shone white and ghostly against the edge of the lake. He smelled tobacco smoke as someone passed outside. He heard a mutter of voices speaking in Farsi. At least he heard, "Stanhope here."

"Get me Ben Kahlmer." His voice was harsher than he meant it to be.

"There is no such person—"

"In Blue Jay 5. K Section."

"Sir, I can't just—there is no—"

"Tell him it's Sam Durell."

"Durell. Yes, sir. Sir—?"

"I'm waiting," Durell said.

"Are you speaking on a clear line?"

"All the way."

"I'm afraid I can't—"

"You'd better."

"Yes, Mr. Durell."

He waited again. Not very long. Ben Kahlmer was K Section's Central in Tehran, a man of economics, a former oil market analyst, a middle-aged man who had spent most of his life exploring Saudi sand dunes for petroleum. He had developed personal financial troubles, and K Section recruited him four years ago by bailing him out at the bank. Kahlmer was grateful for the salvage of his middle age. He had proved proficient and loyal.

"Sam?"

"Ben, I need a relay to Washington. Scrambled."

"No can do, Cajun. Transmissions are heavy, busy, busy. Much ado about nothing, but we're tied up. You'd better give it to me. I'll transmit in about three hours. Did you meet Fingal?"

"I saw him." Durell tried to control his anger. "The little bastard is dead. The hard way."

"Oh, Jesus. Sam, your line is clear—"

"No help for it. What I want from Washington is a new briefing. This thing isn't the simple search-and-deliver chore I was led to believe. Somebody knew Fingal was coming down here to meet me, to give me new data. Somebody ambushed him. It wasn't just a desert amusement, wiping him like that. I don't know what they got out of him, but whatever it was, it was important enough to use extreme prejudice. The poor slob wasn't ready for any of it. He—"

"Are you all right, Sam?"

"Yes."

"You sound funny. Strange."

Durell said, "You tell the boss, Dickinson McFee, back in D.C., that he's sold me down the primrose path. I'm on my back, working in the dark. It was supposed to be simple. It's always supposed to be simple. But Fingal is dead, and that's not easy to accept. Somebody is making me look foolish, and they used Fingal like you'd throw away a burnt match."

"Sam—"

"All right, Ben." Durell drew a deep breath. The phone felt slippery in his grip. "Can you get through to McFee?"

"I told you, three hours. You're sure you want me to tell him all this?"

Durell said, "Ben, I'm supposed to find Nuri Qam, the Second Deputy Minister for Afghani Internal Affairs. He's supposed to be hiding out in Meshed, in Iran. Can you tell me why?"

"No."

"Do you know where to find him, Ben?"

"No."

"Do you know *anything* that Fingal knew?"

Tehran Central hesitated. "It's about the dragon."

"The dragon," Durell repeated flatly. "The one that was in all the newspapers briefly, the item that the Italian archaeologist, Professor Berghetti, dug up?"

"And presumably lost again. Yes."

"It's only an art object," Durell said.

"It's the red button on the bomb, Sam."

Durell waited.

"The Chinese want it, Cajun. A matter of national pride. An excuse to start an incident, maybe. I don't know. I just sit here and mind my own business in Tehran, Sam. I can feel that something big is going on, but I don't know what it is."

"Get McFee to tell me," Durell said flatly.

"Sure. Where will you be?"

"Meshed."

"Why there?"

"To find Nuri Qam, who sent Fingal to fetch me. Why Else? Move your ass on it, Ben."

He hung up.

As he stepped from the back door of the little government building, he saw that Mr. Chadraqi was gone.

Parked at the end of the alley was the van belonging to the three young Americans—Charley, Mort and Annie.

They were waiting for him.

4

"Mr. Durell?"

Charley Anderson pushed the girl, Annie, forward from the van, down the alley toward Durell. She looked back, her dark hair swinging, as if reluctant to move toward him. Their eyes gleamed like those of feral animals in the shadows, catching highlights off the moon. The girl said something he could not understand, as if protesting, and then walked toward him again. He watched the two men. The short one, Mort Jones, balanced his fat body on tiptoe, standing at the rear of the hippie van. Durell saw the shine of his teeth as he grinned. He could not see the man's pudgy hands. Charley Anderson's fingers rested lightly on the front door of the van. The girl came forward.

"That's enough," Durell said.

She stopped. "We just want to talk to you."

"Did you come back to Ur-Kandar just for that?"

"Charley insists we can do business with you."

"We have no business together," Durell said.

"Oh, yes, we have."

She had changed into cleaner jeans and a heavier, checked man's shirt, hanging out over her hips. The night was becoming cool as a wind blew over the briny lake from the northeast. There were no clouds, and the moon, at a gibbous phase, cast a bright light over the little town, as cold and fearsome as the light in the girl's gray eyes. The shadows in the alley were sharp ebony and silver, etching the shape of her delicate nose and chiseled mouth. She seemed to be unarmed. He was not so sure of the two men who waited at a distance behind her at the van.

"What happened to Chadraqi?" he asked.

"Who?"

"The clerk at the inn."

"Oh, him. He ran away."

"Why?"

"He was probably afraid the police would catch him after he allowed you illegally into the government building. Were you using the telephone?"

Durell drew a deep breath. "I think you and your two friends had better just take off. I'm not in the mood for any of your fun and games."

"We just want to talk to you," she said.

"What about?"

"Maybe we took a walk down that ravine after you left us by the road. Maybe we saw things we oughtn't to have seen. Would you believe that?"

He thought of Fingal again. "You found him?"

"Oh, my, yes."

"Who dit it?" he asked.

"Now, how would we know a little thing like that? Was he a friend of yours, Mr. Durell?"

The fat young man, Mort Jones, called something in a soft, impatient, urgent voice. The girl turned her head, her dark hair swinging again, and Durell could have taken her with ease, to use her against the other two, but he did not think they would have any scruples about the girl, and Durell did not want to show any violence yet. It was a half-mile walk back to the inn, and in between was the mosque and the main huddle of mud-walled houses. He had no wish to waken the whole village.

"I don't know what you're talking about," he said.

The girl said, "You're a cold one, aren't you? He was an American, wasn't he?"

"How could you tell?"

"We're just guessing. We've been discussing it a lot. All we know is that we saw your vehicle and saw you coming back up from the ravine. We don't know how long you were down there or why you pegged him out and tortured him. The police would be interested in hearing all this, wouldn't they?"

"Why don't you go to them, then?"

"Well, we're all fellow Americans in a foreign country, aren't we? We ought to stick together, especially in trouble like this." The girl's voice was flat, not very persuasive. "After all, justice here isn't like in the good old U.S.A. They could lock you up and throw the key away, like they do in Turkey—except I think they'd hang you right off the bat. Surely we can come to terms."

"What do you want? Money?"

"Sure," she said. "Lots of it. And a bit more. We could help you, you know."

Mort Jones called again, his voice a hissing sound in the moonlight. The girl did not turn her head this time. When she looked at Durell, he had the feeling again of something behind her eyes; an appeal, perhaps, a cry of anguish. He couldn't be certain. She was one of the trio, a girl who shared herself between the two men. And yet there was an odd discipline here that did not quite fit the pattern of drifting, homeless American youth.

"All right," Durell said, "I'll give you some money, just to save me trouble with the local fuzz, right? We'll go back to the inn."

"No," Mort called. "You come with us."

"Why?"

"We want to show you something. Something that dead man never had a chance to tell you about. Something important. Maybe it's what you were looking for, hey?"

"Like what?" Durell asked.

He felt a menace from the two men more intense than before. The girl stood about six feet away from him and to one side, against the wall of the building, leaving a clear path between himself and the two young men. Somewhere in the village a dog began to bark. It was soon hushed. A camel grunted behind one of the houses across the road that led to the lake. He thought he heard the wailing of a popular Moslem melody; a radio, somewhere. Otherwise, the village was peaceful and quiet.

Mort Jones said, "Tell him, Annie. It's something we don't know what to do about. It's too big for us. We don't want trouble with the cops, either. We can all throw in with each other. Friendly, like. No need to argue or fight about it. You'd lose anyway, buddy. We've got you by the short hairs. So we'll show you this thing, and afterward we can work out a deal, if you've got the right connections." Mort laughed thinly. "Which we think you do. You don't look like one of these businessmen sent over from the States by your corporation. There's a smell about you, mister, that I could catch a mile away. You smell like a cop. But maybe not an honest cop. Maybe you're not above a little deal, anyway."

"I'm not a cop," Durell said.

"Well, you're something," Mort argued. "Anyway, we don't want to hang around here too long. The locals might come sniffing around any minute. So be a good fella, huh? And first off, throw your gun away. We've got you in our sights."

Both men moved slightly, as if on signal, and Durell saw their weapons, snubby automatic rifles that outpowered his .38 beyond any chance of discussion. He was not too surprised. The girl moved quickly out of his reach, drawing back along the wall. All this time, the taller man, Charley Anderson, had left the talking up to the fat boy. Now Anderson spoke, his voice harsh as the desert Durell had left behind.

"You've got ten seconds, Durell."

Durell said, "I'll go with you. But I'll keep my gun, if this is to be a friendly enterprise."

"No. Toss the gun to Annie."

Durell looked at the man's rock-hard face and reached carefully for his weapon and held it flat in his palm, then threw it to the girl. She caught it deftly and backed away some more until she stood with her companions.

"Sensible," Anderson said. "Now get up front in the van, between Mort and me. Annie, you get in the back."

"Where are we going?"

"You'll see."

"What's so big about this that you can't handle it yourselves?"

"We can handle it, all right. But you could tell us something about it. Get in."

They headed southwest, leaving Ur-Kandar and the lake with its shining Greek column behind them. They were on the road back toward the place where Fingal had died. Nobody rushed out to stop them. The sound of the VW van didn't seem to disturb any of the sleeping villagers.

Mort Jones drove. There was an excitation in the fat man that disturbed Durell. Mort hummed, whistled softly, made clucking sounds with his tongue. He did not seem to be high on anything, however. He handled the little bus casually, his fat fingers drumming on the wheel. Now and then Durell felt the muzzle of Anderson's gun grate against his ribs. He felt no desperate alarm as yet. Curiosity about this trio had risen within him to the danger point. Annie sat behind them, clinging for support as the bus jolted on the rough road. Now and them he glimpsed her face in the rear-view mirror. She looked tense and a bit sad, her eyes inward-viewing.

The interior of the van was a surprise. Under the surface clutter of blankets, bedrolls, boxes of equipment that included shovels, rock hammers, and even mountain-climbing gear, the van was scrubbed spotless. The cooking utensils were stainless steel and copper, polished to a high shine, and neatly stowed. The contradiction troubled him. He wondered if it was the girl's influence. Their outward appearance was only a facade. Perhaps Annie was brought up with a sense of tidy housekeeping. But the two men, under their casual grime, were equally meticulous.

The equipment was all relatively new and expensive, some of it from Abercrombie & Fitch, according to the labels. Either they had indulgent parents or their drug-smuggling operation was not as petty as it seemed.

"It looks as if you've been making out pretty well," he said finally.

"We do okay," Charley told him.

"You said you were from Philly?"

"Yes. Philadelphia."

"How long have you been out of the States?"

"Only a couple of months. Mort, we're coming up on it now."

"I know," the fat man said.

"It's to the right, from this direction."

"I know," Mort said impatiently.

Durell said, "How were the Flyers making out when you last heard?"

"They'll never win the pennant," Anderson said. "Just shut up, Durell. If you aren't a cop, you're the next thing to it. Snooping around, estimating what we make, looking at our equipment—" Anderson's gun pushed again at Durell's rib. "We had a job for a while. All three of us. Annie here majored in archaeology at the University of Pennsylvania. Mort was interested in geology until his folks bugged him so much he got rid of them."

Durell turned his head to the driver. "How did you do that?"

Mort Jones giggled. "I killed 'em."

Anderson said, "Cut the shit, Mortimer."

"Well, I did, in a way."

Anderson spoke to Durell. "We had a little job with the Berghetti expedition. Hunting old stuff here, and across the border in Afghanistan. I was straw boss for the gooks. You ever hear of Professor Berghetti? An Italian from the University of Milano. Pretty famous, I gather. Interested in Asian cultures, including China. You're in with that stuff, too. We checked out your hotel room. Two books in Chinese, Tao Tê Ching, and all that stuff in ancient Chinese graphics. Surprised?"

"No," said Durell.

"We were just curious about a guy who murders, that's all."

"I haven't killed anyone lately," Durell said.

Mortimer Jones snickered.

Anderson went on, his voice pedantic, "The old caravan routes used to come out of China and across the Gobi and the mountains and then forked out, some going west, some south to Afghanistan and Iran, which was Persia in those days, and a pretty nifty empire, too. I had long talks with the professor about it. He was looking for the remains of a treasure caravan that belonged to Prince Chan Wei-li, the son of the illegitimate Emperor Shu. The Prince only ruled for eighteen months and tried to establish himself permanently with alliances to the kings of Khwarizm, who offered a few thousand mercenaries to the Emperor to fight the Mongols. Caravans took a long time to travel here, of course. By the time it got here, both the Khwarizm dynasty and the Emperor had been deposed by the Mongols and things were in a mess. The caravan vanished. Had some priceless treasures—jewels, art work, gold, so forth. Sounds like a talltale, doesn't it?"

"These things happened," Durell said.

"Anyway, the professor got some clues from some old Chinese scripts, detailing Prince Chan's treasure, and more hints from some old Moslem scripts he studied in Meshed, and he was digging for the stuff. Annie, Mort and I helped him."

"Did you find anything?"

"We'll show you. Turn here, Mort."

Durell knew he was in deadly danger.

Mort Jones turned suddenly toward an almost invisible goat track that led down through the barrens under the light of the moon. The fat man drove violently, and the turn shoved Durell hard against Charley. Anderson's gun dug cruelly into his side again and the man smiled.

"You know all about Berghetti, don't you, Durell? Your friend—the one we found dead—did he know about the dragon, too?"

Durell said flatly, "What dragon?"

"Come, come, Mr. Durell. None of us are as innocent as we appear, are we?"

The van jolted violently as Mortimer casually took it over sharp rocks and around a hairpin descent. The land here, which fell away to the marshes, was marked by a wide series of gullies, ravines and escarpments descending to the lower altitude of the Hamun Lake system. The wind that came through the van's window was sharp and cold, blowing from the heights of the Mokran. In the moonlight, the land looked empty. Annie muttered something as the van jolted again. This was not the path he had taken earlier to find Fingal's tortured body at the abandoned village. They had only gone about ten miles from Ur-Kandar. He turned to look at the girl. She half crouched, trying to keep her balance against the wild lurching of the vehicle as they ground downhill under Mort's guidance. The girl's eyes were a gray vacuum, sucking light into their depths and giving nothing back. In the flickering light, he saw the two thin Chinese books he had found in Fingal's room, among a scatter of other volumes he could not identify. The corners of the girl's mouth trembled just a bit.

"Did you kill Fingal, Annie?" he asked.

Her voice was bland. "Was that his name?"

"You should know. How long have you been with Charley and Mort?"

"Long enough."

"Which one is better in bed?"

Her voice was flat. "Fuck you," she said.

The VW van jolted to a halt. A cloud of dust and sand boiled up around them briefly. Anderson reached out for the door handle and backed out and away, holding his weapon level.

"Come on out, Mr. CIA man."

Durell did not argue his knowledge. He slid out, facing Anderson, and saw that Mort had stopped the van on a wide ledge of reddish stone, beyond which was a deep drop into a ravine filled with tumbled boulders and the dry bed of a river that didn't seem to have flowed for centuries. The bottom of the little canyon was relatively flat, perhaps forty feet down, with a trail suitable for goats zigzagging down from the ledge. The rim of the moon touched the opposite height of the valley. He heard the VW door slam as Mortimer got out from behind the wheel. The springs of the van creaked. The girl used the rear doors. Durell ignored the automatic weapon in Anderson's hands and walked to the edge of the narrow rock ledge where Jones had stopped the VW.

This part of the country had flourished ages ago, before the deserts crept in and the river dried up. He saw ruins among the boulders, a few ancient columns of serpentine shape, half-shadowed, white against the black where the moon's rays failed to reach. There was a Byzantine look to the ruins, although the village had never been much, and a crude dam dowstream testified to the engineering capacities of the ancients who once flourished here.

"What do you think of that?" Anderson asked.

"Did Professor Berghetti dig here?"

"Hell, no. We found it ourselves and kept it to ourselves. Our private dig, see? We'd take time off from the main search area, which was south of here. The old prof didn't seem to mind when we disappeared."

"You never told him of this place?"

"As I said, we kept it to ourselves. We hoped we'd find the old man's treasure. Of course, we figured most of it was just a pipe dream, but you never can tell." Anderson shrugged his shoulders. "Let's go down. We'll show you what we found."

"I'm not interested," Durell said.

"Sure, you are. That's why you came here, isn't it? You and Fingal. You found something, that's a fact. And that's why Fingal is dead, right?" Anderson's eyes were lost in deep pockets of shadow. "Well, let's go down, anyway."

"If you're going to kill me, do it here," Durell said.

"We just want to show you what we found, and ask what you think of it."

Mortimer Jones had advanced to stare down from the rimrock at the ruins in the valley below. A little smile played on his fat lips. The girl stood a little apart from them, watching and waiting.

Durell said, "You'll never get away with it. I figure

Mortimer is your interrogator, right? He looks like he'd have fun in that sort of work. I guess he did the job on Fingal—cutting away the eyelids, emasculating him, all that. Mortimer tends to go overboard. It wasn't a wandering band of brigands who caught Fingal. It was you three." He turned to the girl. "Anya, did you enjoy watching what Mort did to Fingal?"

She said, "My name is Annie." There was sudden alarm in her eyes. She looked at Anderson. "What's the matter with him, anyway? Doesn't he believe us?"

Anderson said, "He knows."

Durell said, *"Tovarich,* you mentioned the Philadelphia Flyers not winning the pennant. They're not a baseball team. They're an ice hockey team. No pennants for them. Just the Stanley Cup. You had good training, fairly good schooling. But not good enough."

He drew a deep breath. "You're Russian. Soviet agents. All three of you."

5

Mortimer made a hissing sound. Durell watched him with only part of his attention. The man was excitable and vicious, but it was apparent that Anderson gave the orders. Durell was a cautious man, but not one who refused risks. He had not made the statement that exposed Anderson's cover without thought.

"We have to kill him," Mort Jones said.

"No," said Annie.

Anderson said, "Not yet." He looked curiously at Durell. "You don't really know why you are here, do you? They have not briefed you completely?"

"I'd like to know why *you* are here," Durell said. "The Soviets have interests along the Afghani border, of course. So do the Chinese. But this masquerade? This searching for artifacts in the desert? Was it worth Fingal's life?" He looked at Mortimer Jones's sweaty face in the moonlight. "And do you usually work with such freaks, Anderson? Jones is not competent." He switched suddenly, easily, to Russian. "Jones should be eliminated, not I."

Invective, foul and not distinguished by its inventiveness, poured from Jones like trash flowing along a sewer. Durell heard the girl draw a deep, weary breath. But most of his attention was centered on Anderson. The danger would come from that one; Anderson would make the

41

decision. He did not know why they had performed their convoluted charade; it didn't matter, at the moment. Just now, it was enough to consider the simple matter of survival.

Durell had a knife in a sheath fastened to the inner seams of his shirt collar at the nape of his neck. It could be pulled out hilt-first, fitting the palm of his hand in throwing position in split seconds. They had not searched him, except to take the .38, which Anderson had thrust into his wide belt. Durell had been trained in the use of the narrow, vicious blade at the Maryland "Farm" run by K Section, but he decided in that moment not to use it unless they tried to go over him more thoroughly.

Anderson moved his gun slightly. "We go down, *Gospodin* Durell." He jerked his head toward the man called Jones.

"Why? What's down there?"

Jones grinned. "Perhaps the end of your career, Cajun. Yes, we know your code name. It's been in our files for a long, long time. With a red tab attached to it. Which means, as you of course must know, that you are to be handled with extreme prejudice, as I believe your own official phrasing puts it."

The girl said, "But perhaps he can help us."

"Oh, he will, he will." Jones's round head bobbed in pleasant agreement. "This man is a professional, unlike Fingal, who waited too long before wagging his tongue. This man will be more sensible. He is a capitalist mercenary, fighting against the peoples' revolutions. But he is also a pragmatic man, and he will not permit us to go as far as we had to go with Fingal."

Anderson gestured to the ravine. "Go on down."

Durell started forward to the goat track that led to the rocky bottom and the ruined, ancient village. He saw the flicker of an order in Anderson's eyes, an imperceptible nod, and the moment that Anderson used to look at Mortimer Jones was enough for Durell to reach for the knife in its sheath at the nape of his neck.

The moon over the edge of the rimrock cast the fat man's head and shoulders in bright amber light, while the rest of him was swathed in ebony shadow, invisible against the darkness below. It was as if he had been cut in half. As Jones raised his JP-12, the muzzle moved upward into the light, Durell's knife flickered and sped to its mark. The girl screamed. Anderson started a warning sound in his throat that never fully came out. The knife chunked into Jones's right shoulder. The man's gun began to stutter, set on automatic, sending slugs wildly against the moon. At the same moment, Durell crouched low and dived for Anderson, who had made the mistake of standing too close. He felt the man's gun slam frantically against his head as he smashed into the Russian's middle. Anderson went backward, lost his footing, yelled, and lost his balance on the lip of the ledge. He went down, grabbing and pulling Durell with him. At that moment, he heard a belated scream from Jones and glimpsed the man with the knife embedded in his shoulder; Jones fell into the dry riverbed in a series of insane cartwheels. Durell and Anderson went down, too, locked together in a desperate grip. He had no time to think about the girl.

The dizzying fall was checked by shattering bumps and crashes as they hit rock and scrub on the way down. Durell felt something smash into his left leg, slam against the side of his head, crush against his back. The breath was knocked out of him. The fall seemed endless. Then everything exploded in one last brain-shattering jolt and he lay still, not fully conscious. The sky reeled overhead. There was a roaring in his ears. He told himself to get up. He could not get up. He forced himself to roll on one side and his hand came down on something hard, metallic, unlike rock. It was Anderson's automatic. He closed his fingers on it, felt a small tug against him, pulled harder, got his hand firmly on the grip. Pebbles rolled and clattered down around him. He got to his knees. The sky wavered again. The darkness seemed absolute here at the bottom of the ravine. Something small scrabbled away from him at the edge of the rough river bottom. He could not see what it was.

A large and dark object loomed to his right. He slid toward it, his left leg acting strangely, not in complete control. He hoped nothing had been broken. When he was behind the boulder, he paused and sat with his back against the cool rock and drew several long, deliberate breaths. He could not see Anderson or Jones or the girl, but he thought he heard the girl calling in anxious tones down from the top of the ravine. He could not be sure. His ears rang. But after a long minute, he began to feel better.

There were boulders of all sizes and shapes strewn around him. As his eyes adjusted, he saw that he and Anderson, in their desperate grips on each other, had rolled to the dry riverbed, where eons of storm washes had flung gravel and rolled heavy stones in tumultuous heaps here and there. He looked again for Anderson, but could not see the Russian.

The girl was coming down the narrow goat track toward the ruined heaps of foundation stones in the ancient, deserted village. She carried Durell's gun in her hand. He watched her until she passed below the edge of moonlight and merged into the darker shadows down here. Something moved about twenty yards ahead, toward the ruins. Pebbles rattled.

"Leonid? Anya?"

It was Anderson's whisper. Durell sat still, gathering his strength, and checked the Russian automatic. It was loaded, but the safety was still on. Anderson—or whatever his Russian name really was—had had no intention of shooting him. He had meant to leave that business to Jones-Kokin, who enjoyed slow executions. He slipped the safety catch off and made sure there was a cartridge in the chamber. He kept the gun on single-fire rather than automatic. Then he stood up, crouching, and looked over the top of the boulder that sheltered him.

Kokin lay spread-eagled on his back, his body broken by a sharp outcrop of rock on which he had fallen. Anderson crouched beside him, shaking him futilely. Then the dark Russian turned, slid sidewise, and vanished.

Durell wondered about the girl.

It was a dangerous place for hide-and-seek. He moved slowly forward, grateful that his own body functioned at reasonable normalcy now. Using care to make no sound, he drifted from shadow to shadow toward the spot where he had last seen Anderson.

"Durell?"

The whisper came from his right, across the river where the serpentine, broken columns reared up toward the dim moonlight. It was Anya's voice. He did not reply.

"Cajun, be careful!"

There was a note of anxious warning in her words. He did not understand it. Again, he made no reply.

He did not know why she urged caution on him, against her fellow agent. He assumed it was a trap, and moved on. Perhaps a hundred yares down the ravine, the walls of reddish rock turned sharply right, beyond the village ruins. The moon, dipping fast below the edge of the little cliff, made a pattern of silver down there that reflected somewhat up the narrow gorge. It gave him a slight advantage His general direction was toward Mort Jones's body, where it sprawled like a broken sacrificial offering on the sharp rock where he had landed. He felt no regrets about the man's death. Jones had been ready to execute him, or perhaps inflict on him the same horrible torment he had exercised on poor Fingal. A ripple of small, unseen pebbles gritted out from under his left boot. The sound seemed extraordinarily loud in the ravine. He froze in the shadows and listened. There was no response from his hidden adversary. He could not escape by climbing the goat path again; he would be too exposed as a target on the way up to where the van waited. What lay between him and the Russians had to be settled here, in this rocky, ruined place of shadows.

"Anya . . . !"

It was Anderson, calling with a fierce urgency. Durell looked in the direction of the sound, but he could not see the other man. Neither could he spot the girl. He reached Jones's body, waited again, then began to search with quick efficiency in the man's pockets, taking papers, keys, money. There was quite a thick wad of currency in the dead man's shirt pocket. He could not find Kokin's gun. Perhaps Anderson had already retrieved it to replace the

JP-12 Durell had snatched up. As if in answer to the thought, there came a sharp, stuttering series of cracks from across the riverbed. Rock splinters broke and screamed in the dark air. Durell dived behind the boulder and waited, checked the direction from which the shots had come. The place seemed a little farther south than the spot from which Anderson had called to the girl. The dim rectangular ruins of house foundations made deeper cavities of shadow in the blackness over there. The top of one of the Byzantine columns was touched by the fading moonlight. Soon it would be completely dark down here in the canyon.

"Anya, come here!"

The girl did not reply to Anderson's repeated call. Durell started to rise, and again a rapid burst of shots came his way. He dived flat once more, than crawled rapidly on knees and elbows toward the riverbed, slid down the slight depression it made, and rested on the opposite bank. The sand and rock still held the close heat of the past day, but now a wind came whimpering around the far turn of the narrow valley, and he felt a chill in the air.

Something moved among the ruins to his right. A small stone rattled. He heard quick, anxious breathing a bit ahead of him when he turned and crawled up and over the river bank. Nearby was the first of debris-filled cellar excavations. He looked beyond, searching the darkness for Anderson. The broken columns of the old settlement made silhouettes against the far wall of the ravine, where the moonlight was reflected. He dried his palm on his thigh and renewed his grip on the Russian automatic. There was silence.

He listened.

Faintly, faintly, he heard the sound of someone moving in the foundation hole. He slid forward and halted only a few feet from the base of the single twisted column that reached for the moon. He heard nothing for a long moment.

"Anya!"

It was difficult from here to locate the sound of Anderson's call. It could have come from directly ahead, in the rubble-filled excavations, or almost anywhere. The voice bounced off the rocky walls of the ravine and echoed back and forth, confusing each other. The word was laced with anger now, a sense of betrayal because she did not answer him. Then he saw the shape of a head and shoulders rising carefully out of a depression ahead.

He moved fast, rising to his feet, and dived hard for the dim figure. He heard several shots slam back and forth from the canyon walls. He could not tell where they came from. Then he hit the figure in the back, drove the person forward, and knew instantly that he had found the Russian girl. She gave a small cry and fell forward, and he fell on top of her. Her firm body convulsed in involuntary panic. He clapped a hand over her mouth, caught at her wrist, slammed his elbow down on her other arm, and pinned her under him.

"Be quiet," he whispered. "Absolutely quiet."

"Please—"

He spoke in Russian. "If you say one more word, I'll kill you."

She knew he meant it. Her body remained taut under him, then lost all its resistance.

"Anya!"

Echoes went back and forth through the darkness like startled birds overhead.

"Listen to me," Durell said. "Are you listening?"

Her head moved in a spasmodic nod. Her breathing was quick, frightened. He smelled the scent she used in her hair. He said "Answer quietly. Very carefully. Who is Anderson?"

"Like me. An agent. On a mission here."

"What mission?"

"They want the dragon."

"What dragon?"

"The dragon," she repeated.

"Who are *they?* KGB?"

"Nyet. I think not."

"You're not KGB?"

A nod. "I am. Yes. But Pigam Zhirnov? Leonid Kokin? I am not certain."

"That makes no sense."

"No. It does not."

He said, "You tried to warn me against them?"

"Killing you would be senseless."

"That's all?"

"I—I think I need your help. Please. Be very careful. Zhirnov will kill you. He *must* kill you now. It is why he and Kokin brought you here. To question you and to kill you."

"Because of the dragon?"

She nodded, sucked in a breath, was silent. He felt her body all over, careless of the amenities, and recovered his own gun, the S&W .38, from her belt. She seemed to carry no other weapons. He felt better, and released his crushing hold on her.

"Anya!"

The angry-sounding echoes flew about his head.

"Why does Anderson—Pigam Zhirnov—want you?" he whispered.

"He will kill me, too, I think, and blame it on you."

"But you're a team—"

She said, "I think not. I think our purpose here is not what I understood it to be. Zhirnov knows I have become suspicious. It is enough for him, a man like him."

"All right. I'm letting you go. Be very careful."

"Yes."

He rolled away from her and put the Russian gun in his belt, preferring to hold the .38. It felt good and familiar in his grip. The girl did not move for a moment. Then she rolled sidewise, her long hair disheveled and swinging. He could not see her face in the darkness. An arm's-length away, and she would be invisible. He smelled the dust of antiquity in his nostrils from the ancient excavation. He stood up, his head exposed, and looked around.

The moon was gone.

Except for the broken angular strip of starlit sky formed by the walls of the ravine, there was no other light. He reached behind him and caught the girl's wrist. She was momentarily reluctant to leave the illusory safety of their hole, but then she climbed up with him. The wind made her loose shirt flap briefly. He felt her shiver. There was a cluster of broken columns ahead and to the left, ghostly in the light of the stars. He moved that way with care, trying to avoid the rubble of broken building blocks and potholes. He felt as if he were stalking a tiger in the dark of the night. He visualized Zhirnov now, lean and dark and intense, holding the gun, watching and waiting. The presence of the girl with him, the possibility that he might miss and hit Anya when aiming for him, would not stop Zhirnov. Durell pulled her behind the shelter of the three or four rearing columns. Their safety was dubious. Zhirnov could be anywhere, to the right or left or even behind them now, in the narrow, dark canyon.

But he had the keys to the van, and it was a long ten miles back along the dangerous road to Ur-Kandar. Zhirnov had already slipped up there, when he had tried to revive Jones, but he had not found the ignition keys. Durell had them. He looked across the riverbed. He could barely make out the bulk of the van in the starlight. But the climb up the side of the ravine would leave them as exposed as flies on a wall. It was a momentary checkmate. The keys were no good to him unless he could get back up there.

"There," Anya whispered. "There."

He saw nothing in the direction she pointed.

"I thought I saw him moving," she breathed.

"No."

It was a game of patience, one in which he had been well-trained. But then, he was sure that Pigam Zhirnov had equal expertise at this deadly standoff. There was the girl to be considered, too. She was hostile, but at the same time he sensed her need for him, gleaning hints that she was at odds with her own companions. He did not understand this, and for the moment he did not try to.

This time he made the approach.

"Zhirnov!"

His voice echoed. There was no answer.

"Zhirnov! I have Anya! She is helpless and hurt—"

"No," the girl murmured.

He did not loosen his grip on her wrist. He called

again, "She needs help, Zhirnov. Don't you care about her?"

This time he heard laughter, cruelly distorted by the walls of the ravine. He tried to estimate the general direction it came from, and judged it to be farther down the canyon, where the riverbed turned to the right, just beyond the ancient dam that once had blocked and controlled the flow of the stream. He turned his head briefly and looked at the girl.

"Will you stay here? Wait for me?"

She shook her long hair. "No. I come with you."

"All right. Let's go."

"Wait," she insisted.

"He's up there. We're as trapped as he is."

"I know, but—will you kill him?"

"Only if I have to."

"We can escape—move back. We could climb the walls farther back." Her breath was uncertain. "Do not kill him, please."

"I want to question him."

"You can question me. Later. Please. I will be honest with you. I promise. I swear it."

"What do you swear on? Your socialist ideals?"

"I have a God," she said grimly. "My parents were exiled and died for Him. I swear on his Name."

"Do your bosses know about your beliefs?"

"They know about my parents, of course. Perhaps it was necessary to do such things, in the early days. I have no hatred in my heart for those who persecuted us. Just the same, I am faithful and loyal to my country. Make no mistake about that."

"I won't," he promised grimly.

A sudden barrage of shots came from the direction of the dam. The bullets flew overhead like aimless hornets. One of them hit a broken column and sent chips of stone whistling in the air. The girl shivered. He looked back up the ravine. There was a giant tumble of rockfall about a hundred yards behind them, well past the goat track by which they had descended.

He pulled the girl backward with him, moving as silently as possible. No more shots came down the ravine. When they were beyond the village ruins, it was just a short sprint to the tumbled boulders in the neck of the gorge. He kept a grip on the girl's hand when he ran for it. Two shots racketed up and down the canyon. The bullets went wide. In another few moments they were across the riverbed, clambering up the steep slope to the level where the van was parked. They were exposed up here against the starlight, but Zhirnov apparently did not spot them. Or perhaps he was content to let Durell go, thinking that with the girl planted at his side, he might gain his objectives more easily. Durell did not trust Anya in any way. Her behavior seemed sincere, but there was a competent toughness underlying her words and her actions.

It took five minutes to work their way back to the ledge where the van was parked. In that time, there was no sound or movement from the ruins below. The girl slid quickly in beside the driver's seat; he took the wheel himself.

When the engine turned over, the mechanical roar seemed to fill sky and earth. He was sure that Zhirnov would begin to fire at them in his frustration.

But nothing happened. The man had disappeared. Or given up. Or was content that Anya was with him.

He began to feel his aches and bruises from the fall down the canyon side as he backed the van carefully up toward the road above. Before this business was over, he knew there would be another time and another place when he would meet Pigam Zhirnov again. He would settle the score for Fingal when that happened.

6

_____

She said her name was Anya Lubidovna Talinova.
She seated herself in the single chair in Durell's tiny room
in the provincial hotel and sat back, her arms stiffly bent,
pushing her palms against the seat on either side of her
hips. Her manner was defensive. Her eyes were big,
watching him as if he were some strange beast about to
devour her. He wondered what sort of tales she might
have been told about Americans. She did not express any
inner guilt for helping him to escape from her two fellow
agents. Her dark eyes were fathomless as she watched
Durell's every move as he checked out the room.

"We'll have to leave," he said. "Very soon. Zhirnov
knows of this place, so it's no longer safe for you."

"For me?" she asked.

"He will consider you a traitor, perhaps a defector.
You betrayed him back there by helping me to get away.
What else could he think? Your career with the KGB is
finished, Anya. By the way, what is your rank?"

"Lieutenant-Colonel," she said.

He tried to picture her in a military uniform, complete
with shoulder boards and medals. "So young?"

"I've done good work for my country." Her chin was
proud. "I have earned my promotions."

"But you will be suspect from this moment on," Durell

pointed out. "Didn't you consider that, when you chose to help me?"

"Yes, I thought of it."

"Then why did you do it?"

"It was Jones and Anderson—Zhirnov—who were suspect in my mind, for what they were doing, not I."

"What were they up to? What was your team supposed to do?"

She was silent for a moment. Durell moved quietly around the room, checked his bag, then stepped out through the slatted doors to the wooden balcony that ran around three sides of the inner courtyard of the caravanserai. The night air smelled of the briny lake and the reed swamps all about. It felt heavy and warm and sticky in his lungs. The moon was down. When he looked at his watch, he saw it was only an hour before dawn. He could not see his Toyota Land Cruiser, which had been parked in an alcove to the right of the main courtyard gate. The Baluchi caravan men and their women who had camped inside the court all seemed to be asleep. Their charcoal-cooking fires were faint glowing embers, scattered here and there between the recumbent forms. One of the camels snored, loudly and persistently. The wind blew smoke upward from the charcoal fires, across the wooden-railed balcony. There were no lights in any of the other rooms. Nothing stirred. From far off, added to the camel's snores, came the dim barking of a dog.

He stood in the shadows of the long walkway over the courtyard, waited three minutes and then another three minutes, watching and listening. He did not feel alone. He looked up at the brilliant stars, felt the faint, marshy breeze off the lake, heard one of the Baluchi men cough and grunt in his sleep. He went back inside.

Anya had not moved from her position in the crude wooden chair. He knew at once that she had not touched his bag or his papers or his weapons.

"Pigam Zhirnov is out there," she said softly.

"Yes. Somewhere. What were you three supposed to be doing in Ur-Kandar?" he asked again.

"I did not come with you for an interrogation," she

said stiffly. "It is I who should question you, Mr. Durell. You have no business here. Your country has nothing to do with this matter."

"When it comes to that," he countered, "what business do you have here? It seems to me that we're both unwelcome strangers in a strange land." He turned down the hissing gasoline lantern until the room filled with webbed shadows again. He thought he heard someone stir faintly in the cubicle next door. "I think you had better come with me."

"You are not very courteous to someone who saved your life," she said.

"Come along. We'll decide who thanks whom later on. I don't want to leave you here alone."

"Where do you want to go?"

"North. But that's later on."

"North? Where?"

He told her no more than necessary. "You'll know later. Let's go."

"But this place is where—"

She paused. He waited. She said nothing more. He said, "I'm only going to find Mr. Chadraqi."

She got up and followed him from the room.

He found the Toyota where he had left it. The man he had hired to guard it against vandalism and theft was sound asleep in the shadows nearby, but nothing seemed to have been disturbed. Durell let the man sleep, and went next with Anya to her multicolored van. She climbed inside and gathered up clothing while he watched in silence. In two or three minutes she changed into dark slacks, boots and a thin sweater and pulled out a small suitcase of extra wear. He noted the radio and electronic equipment banked against one side of the van, when she pulled away one of the built-in bunks. The Russian team had been efficiently equipped. He watched the shadows, thinking of Zhirnov's bitter, fanatic's face. The man Kokin, who had called himself Jones, had been simply a hired killer; it was Zhirnov who headed the team, until Anya's rebellion broke it up and left him alone. Zhirnov would not be alone for long, however, Durell reckoned; and it seemed to him that every shadow held a menace from the man.

Anya jumped from the rear of the van. "Where do we go now?"

"Come along. You'll see."

"You treat me like a prisoner," she protested.

"That's exactly what you are."

"I could call the police and tell them that you are forcing me—"

"Go ahead. Right now. Tell them everything."

She grimaced. "You know I could not do that."

He walked toward the hotel office. "Did you ever know a man named Colonel Cesar Skoll, in the KGB?"

"Skoll?" She looked at him peculiarly. "Yes. A Siberian. How do you know of him?"

"We worked together, once or twice. Not willingly, but effectively." Durell smiled wryly. "How is he?"

"He is in prison," she said flatly.

"Ah. The freedom of the Soviet Union. What was Skoll charged with?"

"I do not know." The girl was agitated. "As a matter of fact, I am his replacement on this mission. But I do not know the charges against Colonel Skoll, or anything else about the affair."

Durell went into the proprietor's office first. It was dark inside, although now there was a faint illumination in the sky to the east, far away over the lake and the Afghan border along the Helmand and Khash Rivers. The office was empty. The last time he had seen Mr. Chadraqi was when he had left the man outside the government post office, followed by the subsequent attack by Zhirnov and Kokin.

"I have a torch," the girl said.

"Let me take it."

He thumbed the button and carefully swept the dim little office with the beam. Everything seemed normal. There was a curtained doorway in the rear, and he headed for it, hearing the camel cough and snore in the courtyard. The curtain parted with a jingling noise of small bells. It made little difference. He smelled sleeping bodies, heard a quick rustle of clothing, and thumbed the flash again.

"It's me, Mr. Chadraqi. Durell."

"Oh. Very good. Allah is merciful."

"Come out here, please."

A woman's voice queried them sleepily. Chadraqi made soothing sounds and struggled into an old gray robe, put on slippers, and limped into the outer office. He first went to the door and sniffed at the warm dawn air, considered the caravan men in the courtyard, and then turned back to Durell and Anya Talinova.

"You are well, sir? This is most fortunate. I saw those three young countrymen of yours coming after you—"

"They were not my countrymen," Durell said. "I may need more help from you, Chadraqi."

"No, sir, I have done all I could, I have taken great risks that could leave my poor family, my wife and my daughters impoverished and perhaps in prison, at great risk and cost—"

"You will be paid for it," Durell said.

"Ah. Ah, yes. Allah is most generous to the poor, indeed."

"It's not a case of Allah, this time," Durell took money from his pocket, rial notes, and separated a thousand-rial note from his funds. Chadraqi's dark, liquid eyes gleamed with sudden interest, and he bobbed his head.

"Yes, sir. It is not often I have the blessing of opportunity here in this small vilalge—"

"Do you know my Toyota?" Durell asked.

"Yes, of course. Mahmud guards it."

"Mahmud sleeps and dreams of paradise, perhaps. No matter. Can you drive such a car?"

"Yes, sir." Chadraqi was instantly proud. "Yes, I can."

"And you have a daughter, approximately this young woman's age and size?"

Chadraqi stared at Anya curiously. "Indeed, yes. By the blessed hand of Fatima—"

"I would like you and your daughter to take the Toyota and drive it north, through Hormakabad toward Zabul.

I will give you some of my clothes, and your daughter can wear an outfit of Miss Talinova's. Got that?"

Chadraqi nodded, his eyes intelligent. "We are to pretend that we are you, sir?"

"Exactly."

"Through Hormakabad, toward Zabul. Yes. And we go all the way? It is a bad road, sir. Very bad country. Very unfriendly people, who do not respect the teachings of Allah. My daughter is the blessing of my heart, the rose of my eye, the breath in my lungs. I assume there is danger, sir?"

"Yes, there may be danger."

"For myself, the thousand rials is plenty. But for my daughter, perhaps another thousand—"

"Two hundred," Durell said.

"Sir, perhaps more. Eighteen hundred, altogether."

"Fifteen."

"It is agreed. And when do you wish us to go?"

"At once. When you are dressed as I am, and your daughter, the rose of your eye, is dressed like Miss Talinova, you must depart as loudly and as obviously as possible."

"I understand."

"If you are stopped," Durell suggested, "do not argue and do not struggle. Simply come back."

"And who will try to stop us, sir?"

"I do not know."

"And you, sir? Where do you go?"

Durell touched the man's arms. "It is really not necessary for you to know, is it?"

"They will ask," Chadraqi said.

"And you will not know."

"Yes, sir."

Durell led the girl quickly back to the little room. The Baluchi people were already astir in the courtyard in the dim light, although the sun had not yet come up. The air smelled more strongly of the briny lake. He took his bag, checked his gun, and asked the girl for the keys to the van.

"Chadraqi will cheat you, of course," Anya said. "He will drive out of the village, out of sight, and simply wait there for a while, and then come back."

"Perhaps."

"It will not fool Zhirnov."

"Perhaps not."

"And why did you tell Chadraqi to drive north if you intend to go that way, yourself?"

"Because Zhirnov might think that we, in turn, plan to go south. But we're going north, too."

"In the van?"

"Only part of the way. Then south, to Zahidan."

"Ah, yes," she said. "The airfield?"

"Yes."

The girl drove the van with an easy expertise, and her competence put Durell's nerves a bit on edge. In the dawn light, the road to Zahidan was occupied only by a few goatherders, a single camel-train, and once they were overtaken by a local bus that passed them with a blare of the horn and flash of light. As soon as they were away from the lake region, with its swamps and reeds and salty humidity, the desert quickly took over again. In this area of the world, at this time of the year, the average mean temperature stood at 120° normally. Today, Durell thought, it would be hotter than that.

Anya kept watch in her rear-vision mirror, but the rough, narrow dirt road behind them remained empty. There was no obvious pursuit. She looked different than she had yesterday, when she posed as a young American girl traveler. She drove as fast as she could, mindful of the oncoming heat of the day, and her long dark hair blew extravagantly in the wind. Now and then Durell studied her from the corner of his eye, and he knew she was aware of his scrutiny. She had a fine profile, a strong chin, a delicate and aristocratic nose. Her brows were naturally arched, and he doubted if she knew the techniques of plucking and reshaping them. Her underlip was full, almost sensuous, and her long, lithe body was rounded and

womanly where it ought to be. Now and then the van
lurched when they hit a pothole, and he was thrown
against her. He could feel the warmth of her thigh
through the light slacks she wore. They had not briefed
her back in Moscow that it would be more appropriate in
this country of Moslem tradition for her to wear skirts.

After a time he took Homer Fingal's book of Tao poetry from the wide pocket of his bush jacket and studied
it. It was a slim volume in Chinese Mandarin, bound in
well-worn blue leather. Durell's knowledge of Mandarin
was reasonably good enough for a sketchy translation as
he opened it from the right side. The girl at the wheel
gave him a sidelong glance.

"Yes," she said, "your dossier in our files tells us you
are versed in a number of languages. I do not read Chinese, however. Is the book yours?"

"It was Homer Fingal's," he said shortly.

"But Kokin was not certain, when he found it—"

"He doesn't read Chinese, either, I gather. Pay attention to your driving, please."

She looked away, her mouth compressed with dissatis-
faction. Homer Fingal, as an Orientalist, had been competent and scholarly. As an agent for K Section, he had
fumbled and stumbled and eventually fallen into the pit of
death. And yet, Durell thought, there might be something . . .

Most of the little chapters, arranged in a format of poetry, consisted of negatives and contradictions, the teachings of Tao Tê Ching in mystical and often baffling anom-
alies. Fingal had long ago underlined the most puzzling
passages, judging by the pencil smears and well-thumbed
pages of the booklet. Durell read:

> Bend, and you will be straight.
> Be empty, and you will remain full.
> Be old, and you will stay new.
> The Sage keeps to One, and becomes All.

He saw nothing helpful in the phrasing. He read another of the groups of characters:

> Between yes and no there is no difference.
> Between good and evil, is there a difference?
> The ignorant are bright,
> The witty are stupid.
> Tao is a thing both visible and intangible;
> But there is substance and essence in it.

> All things in the Universe come from Being,
> And being from non-being.
> Returning is the movement of Tao
> And weakness is the appliance of Tao.

Durell put down the book for a moment. He saw nothing but obscure scholarly academics in Homer's little book. Yet he had carried it with him to the rendezvous where he had met his death. The old underlinings meant nothing. Did the fact that it was simply Chinese have importance? That alone could be Homer's message. Homer Fingal was supposed to have instructed him on how to find Nuri Qam, the Afghan Deputy Minister who had handled the case of Professor Berghetti and the *objet d'art* that was known as the Afghan dragon. Were the Chinese in on it as well as the Russians?

He read:

> As Tao is to the world,
> So are streams to the rivers.
> The rivers become kings, rising and lowering.
> Therefore the Sage, to be above the people,
> Must keep below them.

Another bus went by, coming from Zahidan. This one was crowded with locals, almost all men, their heads and bodies wrapped in ragged clothes against the dust. Anya had to pull off the road to let the juggernaut go by; there was no room on the narrow path for both vehicles. She clashed gears nervously as she started up again. The sun topped the edge of the plain to the east, and the first hot shafts struck the open pages of the Tao Tê Ching book. It was then, in the slanting light, that Durell saw the thumbnail marks made by Fingal under certain passages.

> The city of Tao is to the north.
> The net of heaven is vast and wide,
> But nothing escapes wisdom.
> In the palace of the Sage there are no walls.
> In the house of Tao there were many windows.
> But no one truly lives there.

Durell closed the blue leather book. Homer Fingal might have been an erudite academician, more suited to library stacks than this cruel and brutal land, but he had managed to do his job. To the north was Meshed, a holy city. It was noted for its bazaar, a place of no walls and many windows, where the merchants did not live, but only carried on their trade.

He knew where to go.

7

He was in luck. There were two flights a week on a feeder line of Iran Air that flew from Zahidan to Meshed in the *ostan* of Khorasan, and they had hit the right day. Anya had no objection as Durell bought their tickets, producing their papers for the lackadaisical clerk. Meshed was less than one hundred miles from the USSR border. Their flight was scheduled to leave at 0945. It was a flight of about 700 kilometers, and Durell figured that the approximate 400 miles could be covered in less than two hours, bringing them to Meshed about noon. They had almost an hour in which to wait, and they cleaned up in the primitive facilities available. He was a bit concerned about letting her out of sight, but she seemed as anxious to accompany him as before. There was a teahouse near the airfield, and Durell bought breakfast for them, paying less than fifty rials, and then got extra cups of hot tea, although the sunbaked airfield thermometer already registered 105°. Somehow, Anya managed to remain cool and fresh-looking. She bought a silk scarf for her long dark hair, and did not offer to share the expense of the plane fares when Durell paid for the tickets. White-necked crows perched on the telephone lines, and an occasional bus wheeled recklessly in and out of the airfield parking area. Durell put the van in the least conspicuous place he could find. The dust of their drive had obscured both the faded designs and the license plates. He locked it up, although he did not expect much to be left of the vehicle after the usual thievery of tires, wheels, and anything removable.

"Was there something you wanted to save out of it?" he asked the girl.

"No. Nothing. I never want to see it again. It stinks of Kokin. I don't want to remember him."

"But you were part of the team," he said.

"I did not kill or torture your friend Fingal. I was left behind on the road, away from it all, to keep watch. I did not know what Zhirnov and Kokin planned to do."

She turned away and sat down on a crude bench in the shade beside the hangar. Mechanics nearby were working on several planes, and there was a slight stirring of activity in the hangar shed as the bi-weekly flight was prepared. The girl's face was somber as she regarded Durell.

"I am afraid of Zhirnov. I do not wish to be a failure in this mission, but I think that you and I, from our different nations, are only pawns in this matter. Our enemies are the same. We are being used as bait for bigger fish, and that is why I have left Zhirnov."

"Were you lovers?"

She grimaced. "No."

"Are you married?"

"No."

"No men at all?"

"That is no concern of yours." She sounded almost prim. "Are you not listening to me? Zhirnov, Kokin and I were sent out together, but I do not think we are employed by the same people. You and I have perhaps the same objectives. But the agencies we each work for have other goals, I think."

"You're being ambiguous."

"Perhaps." She shrugged. "I can explain no more."

"You can tell me what's so damned important about this little dragon."

"The dragon is only an excuse, this statue from old

China. An excuse to blow up a small incident into a large war. It is encouraged by elements in your country and in mine, as well as in Peking."

"Do you know where the dragon is?"

"If I did, I would not be sitting here, not knowing what to do."

"Just what happened to Professor Berghetti, who found the thing in the first place?"

She shook her head and got up and went into the hangar. He followed her, but she only bought some local cigarettes and came back to the bench, blinking in the hot glare of morning sunlight. She struck a match to the cigarette and inhaled deeply, blew out the smoke, and looked gloomily at the waiting plane.

"I am sorry," she said. "You seem to know where you are going and what you must do. I do not. Not any more. I must make some important decisions, and I am not prepared to do so, as yet."

"Berghetti," he urged her.

"Oh, he found the statuette, along with other old artifacts, in the Afghan area of the Seistan, near Qali-i-Kang. Berghetti was a foolish old man. He tried to smuggle it out across the border, but he was intercepted and arrested, and Pasha Nuri Qam, the Interior Deputy Minister, took charge of the case, claiming the art objects for Afghanistan. It all came out in the newspapers. Berghetti refused to tell where he had—how do you say it?—cached the dragon. Peking, of course, immediately claimed the objects and made very threatening pronouncements. But Berghetti himself, we think, was helped to escape from the jail by Mr. Nuri Qam, in order to retrieve the dragon from where the professor had hidden it. Since then, Qam has fled—he took an enforced vacation from his offices in Kabul—and he is believed to be in Meshed." The girl crushed out her cigarette. "So we are going there, is that not so?"

"Yes."

"You know Nuri Qam?"

"We went to the same university, back in the States. We were classmates."

"Ah. Yale, I think?"

"You've been briefed about me," Durell said.

"A little. We know more than you think. You are to find Berghetti, wherever he hides, retrieve the dragon, and give it back to the Afghan authorities, namely Nuri Qam. As a gesture of goodwill, international cooperation, yes?"

"Yes."

"But it is not so simple, my friend."

"I realized that when Fingal was killed by your team. Why do *you* want the dragon? What's the USSR to do with it?"

"If I knew that, I would know why Colonel Cesar Skoll, my supeiror, is imprisoned and taken from this mission. I would know what Zhirnov's and Kolin's true orders were and why all this is so important to Moscow and Peking and Washington."

"But you don't know," Durell said flatly.

"No. I feel that something is very wrong in this matter of the dragon, and that you and I are being used as fools by people in both our countries whom we would not approve of."

"When did you last see Skoll?"

"He was arrested over two weeks ago."

"He's not a man who would care for prison," Durell said. He remembered Cesar Skoll very well, from assignments in Malta and Morocco and Ceylon, where in the past their paths had crossed, mostly as competitors and deadly enemies, and sometimes as unwilling allies. He admired Skoll, had been amazed at the man's brute strength, his quick wit, his unswerving honesty and dedication, his roaring laughter. Colonel Skoll was not a man who would go down easily.

Powerful forces must have been at work to remove him from this mission. Perhaps equal forces were at work back in Washington, controlling and manipulating his own efforts.

A loudspeaker announced their flight. Durell picked

up his bag and motioned Anya to her feet. In the ram-shackle waiting room, he saw the other passengers for the first time. There were no more than eight of them: an elderly German tourist and his tall, languorous blond young bride. There were two youthful Iranian officials, who despite the morning heat wore their dark coats and neckties as emblems of their office; a Chinese of uncertain age, wearing a white Panama hat; an Indian, very dark, with angry, defensive eyes; and two American business-men, sharp and alert, carrying their attaché cases as if they were boarding a commuter train from Manhattan to Greenwich.

The Chinese bobbed his head and smiled affably at Durell. He mentally flipped through the dossiers of Peking's Black House agents, but the man's face rang no bells. The blond German wife gave Durell a direct, appraising look; her stout husband grumbled in Ger-man about the heat.

Durell and Anya trailed after the little group.

"One more thing about your boss, Skoll," he said. "Did you have a chance to speak to him before coming here with Zhirnov and Kokin? Did he give you any hint as to why he refused the mission and was subsequently arrested?"

She frowned. "Only briefly. Skoll is old-fashioned, you see. He feels protective toward women, despite feminine freedom in socialist society. He only told me to be very careful."

"In what way?"

"He suggested that Zhirnov was—headstrong? And apt to cause unnecessary difficulties. Skoll had nothing but contempt, of course, for Leonid Kokin. A mere as-sassin."

"Did Skoll *expect* to be arrested?"

"Oh, yes. He was clearing out his desk when we last spoke to each other."

"But he didn't tell you directly what it was all about?"

"No, he did not."

Durell followed the girl into the Iran Air jet.

8

Meshed was a place of fruits and farms, of minarets spiraling high over holy places, the Imam Reza's
mausoleum, of pilgrims on their way to the tomb of
Nadir Shah and the sacred enclosures where all non-
believers were forbidden. Meshed was a garden exud-
ing the scent of growing things and possessing the aura
of religious fervor that amounted to a strange ecstasy.
It was a quiet storm, fed by the Shi'ite feasts, under a
milder sun than in the Seistan; a storm like the swift
rippling movement of a whirlpool.

Here were memories of barbarians and the glory of
the Sassanids, of nomad wars and the monstrous ava-
lanche of the Mongols led by Genghis Khan, who left
behind them fire and destruction and mountains of
bleached skulls. Meshed was the Place of the Martyr,
where the Imam Reza confronted the Caliph Harun el
Rashid in a conflict between orthodoxy and Shi'ism.
Pilgrims to the holy places in Meshed bring in a tide of
money, coins and rugs and goats to sell, with which to
make their pious offerings.

There were modern things today, however: sugar refineries and parks, traffic circles and broad boulevards,
avenues shaded under gentle trees, and bazaars selling
turquoise and embroidered skin coats, soapstone plat-

ters, rugs, antiques, clay tablets and beads for the religious pilgrims.

Over all lay the heat of summer, which still drove the inhabitants to sleep on their flat roofs and terraces in search of a cool breeze from the mountains toward Quchan.

Among the other passengers in the plane from Zahidan, only the young German woman with her older husband showed any interest in Durell and Anya. She was statuesque and full-fleshed, a modern Valkyrie with long blond hair done up in a tight, sedate braid atop her head; her hands were long and strong, free of jewelry, not even a wedding ring. She did not exchange anything more than monosyllables with her businessman husband, who was engrossed in corporate tallies taken from his attaché case. Durell was aware of her pale gray eyes straying his way, and so was Anya. Anya seemed annoyed. But Anya was interested in the Chinese and the others, as if wondering which, if any of them, could be working with Zhirnov—or perhaps Peking. The blond woman got up once and bumped her soft, pliant hip against Durell's shoulder as she made her way to the back of the plane. She apologized most profusely, first in German that identified her to Durell's ear as a Berliner—West or East? he wondered—and his guess was verified when she gave her name as *Frau* Hauptman-Graz. She waved a negligent hand toward her husband, who was engrossed in his business papers.

"My husband, Hans, he is not a tourist. But I am." When she smiled, her teeth were strong and white and rapacious. "You are touring this part of Asia, also?"

"Yes, indeed," Durell said.

"Meshed is supposed to be a beautiful city, filled with a religious excitement, I hear, an air of holiness, *nicht?*"

"Yes, perhaps."

"And perhaps we shall meet there at the sights to see. *Bitte?*"

"It would be delightful."

She pouted, towering over Durell in his seat like some Norse goddess seeking her prey. "My husband

Hans, he is always busy, I am often lonely and need—companionship? A guide? It would be pleasant to share experiences in Meshed with you and your lovely wife."

Anya said hostilely, "We are not married."

"Ah. So? Well, times have changed, of course—"

"Are *you* married?" Anya asked pointedly.

The blond woman turned slightly pink. "I do not wear Hans's ring, but that is only because—"

An announcement from the cockpit broke it off. The woman sat down again next to her husband and stared out the small window. Anya considered her hands. "The bitch," she murmured. "But then, I suppose you find it commonplace, a man like you is attractive to a certain type of woman—"

"You could have been kinder. She's from East Berlin. Her accent gives her away. A good Communist, no doubt, like you," Durell suggested.

Anya shrugged. "Not all Communists are 'good.' "

"And not all of them follow Moscow's line, is that it?" Durell murmured.

"I do not understand."

"The Black House in Peking would hardly send conspicuous Chinese into Afghanistan and Iran to hunt for the dragon. They would use Maoist fellow travelers who would stand out less against the color of the local people," Durell said. "Like the Indian, up ahead. Or perhaps the two men who look so American, behind us."

Anya was a bit pale. "I did not think of that."

"Do so, then," Durell said.

Not once had *Herr* Hauptman-Graz looked up from his business papers. It was a bit too obvious. They were amateurs. But then, Durell supposed, you can't always be sure of quality when you have to hire outside help.

They were followed from the airport in Meshed. The sun was hot and glittering, and there was a thin haze of pale golden dust in the air. The rest of the passengers scattered and vanished in the waiting room, seeking taxis or being met by friends for the trip into the center

of town. Durell chose a cab and had the driver take
them to the bus station on Tehran Avenue, where he
and Anya then chose another taxi down Pahlevi Avenue, past the banks and the HOMA air office. The
same black Mercedes that had picked up *Herr* and
Frau Hauptman-Graz at the airport doggedly clung to
their trail. It was so obvious that Durell wondered if
there was a second-layer surveillance team, hiding
beyond the Germans. But if there were, he couldn't
find it, nor could he spot a parallel team on the side
streets.

He ignored the Pars and Darbandi Hotels and the
Kousravi Nou, and told the second driver to go out Jahanbani Road, where more modest quarters were
available. After the first twenty minutes, the Mercedes
seemed to have lost them, but he didn't count on it.
Anya sat stiffly, her back very straight, staring ahead as
they rode.

The hotel he chose was small and reasonably clean,
on a side street off Kousravi Nou. Not more than eight
blocks away was the sacred enclosure of the Imam
Reza shrine, the Gauhar-Shad mosque, and the great
bazaar catering to pilgrims and tourists alike, although
the latter were hardly made welcome. There was a privacy to this Shi'ite fervor that made the exclusion of
foreigners more than a bit obvious.

They ate lunch at the Safa, down the street from
the hotel in a narrow lane where traffic could be
watched. He did not see the Mercedes again. They ordered tea from the huge samovar that bubbled on the
zinc counter, and *chelo kebabs,* rice heaped high on a
platter with a sauce of walnuts, the *kebabs* of chicken
skewered and broiled over a charcoal brazier. The
place was smoky and noisy with local inhabitants.
Durell chose a table against the wall, where he could
see the open doorways in the narrow lane and watch
who entered and left. He did not see the Hauptman-
Graz couple. Anya behaved nervously, her eyes rarely
meeting his. She started to talk about Zhirnov, and
wondered what might have happened to her boss, Col-

onel Skoll, but he cut her off, not knowing who might understand English at the crowded tables near them. She looked at him worriedly and picked at her food. Durell found himself ravenous and cleaned up his plate, ordered a bottle of Iranian wine, and ate the flat Moslem bread, and thrust a handful of nuts from the bowl on the table into his pocket.

"Surely," Anya said finally, "you have a special purpose in coming to Meshed?"

"Yes."

"You do not trust me to tell me about it?"

"I want you to stay in the room. Don't answer any knock on the door unless you are sure it is me. Don't go out, don't use the telephone."

She smiled tiredly. "I am confused," she admitted. "I have betrayed my mission, made an enemy of Zhirnov, for saving your life. Why did I do it?"

"Perhaps you have a conscience," Durell said.

"But my own life is destroyed. I do not know where to go, where to turn."

"Stay with me," he said.

Her mouth was wry. But he thought it was a very ripe and promising mouth. She said, "I am alone now. I cannot appeal to my own people. If the German couple are what you say they are, agents of the Black House in Peking, then they are after me, too. What am I to do? Seek political asylum in your country?"

"There are worse choices, Anya."

"No," she said firmly. "I am Russian. I am a Soviet citizen, a loyal citizen. If Zhirnov is working for traitors —hawks, if you like—then I must do what I can to stop him and take my chances with my superiors when I return to Moscow."

"Stick with me," Durell said. "We have the same goal in mind, for the most part. We can help each other."

"How can I be helpful? By remaining locked up in a tiny hotel room? Let me go with you, please, for whatever you have in mind."

She looked lovely and appealing, he thought. But it

was in the nature of his business never to take anything on face value. True, she had saved his life from Zhirnov. But then he wondered about it. The whole thing could have been a subtle arrangement to place her at his side, to put her in his hands, seemingly. He felt a brief rage at what the business had done to him. He had to live with convoluted suspicion, acting out a chess game of mistrust in which move and countermove made endless progressions, until they were alone, totally and irrevocably, cut off from the ordinary, open intercourse which most men enjoyed and took for granted. When he looked into the girl's apparently candid eyes, he felt a rebellion against what his years in the business had done to him. He sipped his hot tea with care—you didn't drink ordinary water in these parts.

"Please, Sam," she said again.

"No," he decided.

The room looked secure enough. There was a solid bolt on the door and the single window opened on the sheer side of the building above an alley. There was a common bathroom at the end of the hall, and he waited until Anya had freshened up in there. The double bed seemed clean enough, with brass head and footboards. A single light bulb dangled from a cord in the ceiling. It was not the most plush hotel in Meshed, but it seemed safe enough.

"Two hours," he promised. "I'll be back by then."

"I shall wait."

He paused in the narrow corridor until he heard her bolt the door, then went down the rickety stairs to the crowded, noisy street. He walked to the Kousravi Nou and turned right to the traffic circle where it met Tehran Avenue. The Imam Reza shrine now loomed to his left. In the early hours of the afternoon, the heat of late autumn had built up until traffic was dampened somewhat, although the ubiquitous taxis, crowded with numerous fares, were still in evidence everywhere. He ignored several and kept walking. Ahead was the sacred enclosure, forbidden to foreigners, although he could visit the famous museum

and glimpse the Gauhar-Shad mosque. He went along
with the tide of fervent pilgrims headed that way, aware
of his being an alien here, conscious of his height and obvious Western origin. Now and then he caught a hostile,
angry face from some devout Shi'ite who resented his
presence even here on the crowded boulevard. He had no
intention of trespassing. His mind kept reviewing the
thumbnailed passage in Homer Fingal's blue bound copy
of the Tao Tê Ching, and he knew exactly where to go.

But it was not that easy.

He did not see the Mercedes that had followed him
part way from the airport, but suddenly he felt the warm
pressure of a breast against his arm and a hand slipped
through to his elbow.

"*Herr* Durell! How fortunate we meet again here in
this enchanting place! You are not with your wife? And I
am not with my husband! So. We shall be tourists together, yes?"

It was *Frau* Freyda Hauptman-Graz. She was as tall as
he, and her grip was strong on his elbow. She wore a pale
gray suit that went with her ice-gray eyes, and a pink
gauzy scarf over her head like a veil, in deference to
Moslem habits. Her makeup made her look like a pho-
tographer's model.

"Come," she said. "Come with me."

"Your husband won't mind?"

"*Ach,* he is always absorbed in his business. It is ma-
chine tools, you know. He lives and breathes lathes and
stamping machines and drill presses. He has so little time
for me! So little inclination. His juices have dried up, I
think."

She matched his stride easily as they turned toward the
great bazaar just below the shrine off Safavi Avenue. He
scanned the traffic for the Mercedes, but could not spot it,
nor could he detect any shadowers in the crowd of pilgrims that surged along with them. Perhaps she thought
she was competent to handle him alone—one way or the
other.

"This way," she said. "It is so nice to see you privately

like this. Without your wife—who says so emphatically that she is *not* your wife. You have traveled far together? Where did you meet? She does not seem to be as American as you, dear *Herr* Durell."

"Annie is fine, but she's a bit tired. She's resting."

"Ach, but you are not in any of the major hotels. Most of them are so—so uncertain, here in Meshed. You must be staying with friends?"

"In a manner of speaking."

She frowned behind her veil. "I do not truly understand you. Perhaps my English is defective. You have friends in Meshed?"

"I wouldn't call them friends. Associates."

They had entered the bazaar area, and were swamped in a tidal wave of noise, the clamor of bells and the cries of hawkers, the shouts and arguments of dickering buyers and sellers. The little shops were all open to the street, displaying their wares of copper and brass, turquoise jewelry, rugs, lambskin coats, Japanese transistor radios, even motorcycles. The smells of coffee, tea and spices mingled with the dung of little donkeys and the ever-present odor of urine. He remembered the thumbnailed phrasing in the Tao Tê Ching: *a house without walls, a home where no one lives.* Somewhere here in the bazaar, in one of the shops, was the contact Fingal had tried to lead him to. To search for Nuri Qam in Meshed without such a lead was all but impossible. He knew that K Section kept a listening post here, close to the USSR border, in a silversmith's place in the southeast corner of the great bazaar, but he had no intention of leading *Frau* Freyda there.

"Ah," she said. "This looks interesting. Let us stop here a moment, *bitte.*"

He was aware of her large leather handbag looped over her right arm as they paused in front of a rug seller's mart.

"In here," the blond woman said.

"I'd rather not. I have no interest in rugs."

"Bitte," she said again.

He was interested to see how far she would go, and now he found out. She dipped her hand into the bag and pressed it against his side, under his arm, and he knew the undeniable sensation of having a gun shoved tightly into his ribs.

"I ask you politely," she said, and smiled.

"A gun is not polite."

"Inside. Quickly."

9

He did as he was told. He had his own .38 in his waistband, and he did not intend to give it up. The dealer in carpets, a Khorasan farmer turned merchant, was haggling with a pilgrim trying to sell a Shiraz rug in order to make an offering at the holy shrine. The bazaar man simply nodded to Freyda and went on bargaining. The blond woman urged Durell into the darker shadows at the rear of the open stall, which was curtained by more carpets hanging on horizontal display poles. She had been here before and knew the way. It was like a maze, moving between the corridors of dusty carpets, but Freyda kept close behind him, the gun in his ribs urging him on.

Finally he came to a wooden wall and a wooden door. Freyda reached past him and knocked briefly in a sharp, coded series of taps. The door was opened immediately. Beyond it was a small room, a cubicle made of rough boards like a shed behind the bazaar rug shop. Part of the room was piled with small three-by-five Baluchi carpets and *poustines,* the locally embroidered lambskin coats and vests. The Chinese gentleman who had been on the plane from Zahidan sat on a pile of the coats. *Herr* Hans Hauptman-Graz sat on the pile of rugs. Both men stood up as Freyda ushered Durell inside and closed the plank door behind them.

"Good," said the Chinese. "You have brought him. But he is still armed, is he not?"

Hauptman-Graz said gutterally, "Your gun, *Herr* Durell."

Durell leaned back against the wooden wall. "You people are damned inefficient. I assume, Mr.—?" He looked at the Chinese.

"Chou. Mr. Chou."

"From the Black House?"

"As you wish. Give the lady your gun."

"Nonsense," Durell said. He had his hand on the .38 tucked into his waistband under the safari coat. "If she fires, I can still get off one shot at you. Depend on it. I won't miss. She should have asked for it earlier, outside."

Freyda made a clucking sound. "There were so many pilgrims in the crowd, Mr. Chou—"

The Chinese smiled. "Never mind. After all, we do not wish to have violence here. We are not on a mission that requires such activity. I am sure Mr. Durell will be amiable in our discussion. He will tell us what he is up to and why, and what he has done with the dragon that rightfully belongs to the Chinese People's Republic as a national treasure. Will you not, Mr. Durell?"

"It depends. Why do you want it so badly? I understand it was found in Afghanistan. After seven centuries, I should think it belongs to the finder. It is an Afghan national treasure now, I should think."

Mr. Chou said softly, "Our new deputy chairman is a man obsessed by our past heritage. He has requested that it be returned to Peking. Diplomatic representations have been made to Kabul, with no reasonable response as yet. If we can simply—obtain—it, there will be no difficulty at all."

"And if you don't get it that way?"

"Diplomacy is the art of arguing with a gun in your hand, after all." Mr. Chou shrugged. He was short and stout, with thick black hair tinged with silver above his ears. He wore silver-rimmed round glasses that gave his face an owlish, benign look. But there was nothing beneficent about him, Durell knew. Anyone from the Black

House in Peking was a mortal factor to be reckoned with. Mr. Chou said, "Where did you find the dragon? And what do you intend to do with it, sir?"

"I haven't found it. But I intend to," Durell said. "When I do, it goes to the Kabul government in Afghanistan. After that, it's none of my affair or my government's concern."

Mr. Chou said patiently, "We know all about you, Mr. Durell. Your code name is 'Cajun,' is it not? We know that you are on loan, so to speak, from Washington, at the request of your old friend, Nuri Qam, to help the Afghanis recover the dragon. I warn you, our Deputy Chairman means to have it. There will be no equivocation about the dragon. One way or another, at whatever cost, he will have it in Peking. It is not important in itself, of course. We both understand that. And it is not the concern of your country. True, the Russians—certain of them—would like to irritate the Deputy Chairman into making aggressive moves. It could certainly be done." Mr. Chou spread his hands, and Durell could see in the gesture the deadly mushroom clouds of a thermonuclear holocaust. "A showdown between the legitimate claims of the Chinese People's Republic for Siberian territorial adjustments and the nationalist, imperialist expansionist aims of the deviationists in Moscow may certainly become inevitable. Would you want that? Of course not. No reasonable man would destroy the world for such foolishness. So be reasonable, Mr. Durell. We three—*Herr* and *Frau* Hauptman-Graz and myself, are not the totality of the forces at work to prevent you from taking the dragon to Nuri Qam. Your trust, in any case, is misplaced. Mr. Qam has his own ideas as to the eventual disposition of the art objects. You would be better off to cooperate with us."

"I don't have the dragon," Durell said flatly.

"Come, come."

"Not yet," Durell added.

"Ah. But you have learned where it is?"

"Perhaps."

"Tell us, then," Mr. Chou said gently.

"To hell with you and the Black House and your nuclear threats and your new Deputy Chairman."

"You are angry, I see. But it was not we who tortured and killed your friend Mr. Fingal. That was the work of the Russians. That perverted man, Kokin. Do not blame us for that."

Durell was silent. Freyda emphasized the pressure of her gun in his ribs. The big blond woman looked eager to pull the trigger. She would have done well in Nazi times, he reflected. Her stout little husband also produced a gun, a Luger, and pointed it at Durell.

Durell said, "And what if I don't cooperate with you?"

"All men are mortal," Mr. Chou said. "We must all face death sooner or later. But better later, I should think, than now, at this moment. I am not a patient man, contrary to your Western concept of Orientals. If I cannot get the dragon from you, I shall retrieve it from your pretty Russian companion, Miss Talinova. Yes, we know about her, too. And Pigam Zhirnov. And the sadist, Kokin. We are efficient. We can be ruthless. And at the moment, I am impatient."

Durell suddenly knew that Chou would not let him leave this little room alive. The red tab on his dossier in Peking made him fair game for killing by any Black House agent.

It was stiflingly hot in the plank shed behind the carpet dealer's shop. The sound of crowd noises from the bazaar were muffled by the multiple layers of carpets that hung outside the door. A shot, or several shots, would surely go unnoticed and unheard by those outside. There were no windows in the wooden room, but the walls seemed to have been knocked together from thin plywood crates. There were no other doors except the one by which he had been forced to enter.

"So, Mr. Durell?"

Freyda was breathing faster than normal in her eagerness, and she pressed the gun closer to him. He said, "All right," and then shrugged and turned inward toward her, forcing her to shift the gun in her hand. The next moment, with exaggerated care, he removed his .38 with two

fingers from his waistband. Mr. Chou sighed and smiled.
Freyda looked at the Chinese and Durell made his move
the moment she shifted her gaze.

His gun slammed a single shot at Hauptman-Graz,
who happened to be the nearest target, and in the same
moment, he used his left arm to drive Freyda's gun away
from his body. It went off a split-second after his own
shot, and the double roar seemed deafening in the tiny,
closed room. The Luger's slug went wild. The woman
squawked and shouted something in German as she saw
her husband topple backward off the pile of rugs. Mr.
Chou came off his seat of *poustines,* holding a gun.

Durell dropped down, sliding forward on one knee,
fired at the Chinese, missed, and his shoulder knocked
Freyda down in a tumble atop him. Her flesh was soft and
yielding. Mr. Chou had no qualms about his target. His
gun crashed and Durell felt Freyda jerk as the bullet
grazed her, aimed at Durell. The woman's Luger fell to
the floor. Durell came up and hit Chou in the stomach
with his head. The man fell backward, upsetting the balanced pile of embroidered coats and vests. He became
entangled with them for a moment, and Durell heard
Freyda swear softly in German, saw her grope for her
fallen gun, and waited no longer.

The plank door to the rear of the carpet shop was not
locked. Durell drove through it, found himself in the
maze of hanging carpets dependent on their long bamboo
poles across the back of the shop. A bullet thudded
through them from behind as Chou recovered his balance.
Durell dropped flat, urged himself on hands and knees
under the hanging rugs rather than to try to fight his way
through the narrow passages they formed. The carpet
dealer had concluded his haggling with the pilgrim and
was alone in the shop. He stared at Durell with mouth
agape. Durell wasted no time on him. He ran for the front
of the shop and the crowds of people in the great bazaar.
The place was a rat's nest of alleys and lanes, each one
devoted to special crafts—coppersmithing, jewelry, more
carpets, clothing. Shouts and pleas and arguments filled
the hot afternoon air, but the deep lungsful Durell drew

felt relatively cool after the sweaty heat in the little room behind the carpet shop.

He shoved his way rapidly through the motley crowd. Looking back, he saw Chou and the woman come out after him; he moved faster, but not too fast as to attract the attention of someone in the crowd or of the occasional uniformed policeman who patrolled casually through the bazaar. Members of the crowd, motivated by their intense religious fervor, would gladly seize the opportunity to mob him, recognizing him as an obvious *ferengi,* a foreigner.

It was not until he reached the first corner that he noticed two others closing in on him. From the minaret of the Gauhar-Shad mosque came the sudden ululations of a muezzin, calling the faithful to prayer. The cries were amplified by loudspeakers and inspired a tidal wave, sending all the Moslems in the crowd for their prayer rugs. The two men at the corner were Afghans, dressed in tribal costume—big men, with fierce moustaches, heavily muscled under their white shirts. They hesitated, aware of the fact that they would stand out in the vast crowd if they refused the call to prayer that boomed out from the minarets. Finally they responded by crouching in the proper position. For Durell, fortunately, there was an open shed where a jeweler practiced his craft on local turquoise stones. He stepped quickly inside, out of the crowded, dusty lane. Behind him, he saw Chou hesitate. Freyda, heedless of local customs, kept coming on, a vengeful Valkyrie in a sea of prostrate forms.

Durell made his way to the back of the jeweler's stall. The merchant glared angrily at him and raised a brief shout, and then subsided as the muezzin's call from the minaret clamored brazenly again. A curtained doorway led Durell swiftly into a back lane.

He turned right, thankful to see no one here, and ran a distance down the lane until he saw a second doorway, this one of wood, and pressed against it. It was open. He looked back just as the curtained exit began to open outward with Chou's pursuit. Chou did not see him. He found himself in a back storeroom that smelled redolently

of spices. The darkness inside was broken by a thin film
of light beyond the kegs and barrels stacked to the ceiling.
He listened, moved forward, heard voices suddenly re-
sume bargaining, and walked through into the shop from
the back way. The shopowner was busy with a client;
neither man noticed him. He slipped out and went to the
right again, seeking the Way of the Silversmiths.

Prayers were over as suddenly as they had begun, and
the crowded alleys resumed business as usual, Now and
then he looked back as he took one twisting lane after the
other. Towering high over the jumble of sheds and shops
were the minarets of the mosque and the bulk of the museum, the only building at the sacred enclosure not denied
to foreigners. It contained Shi'ite Islamic art, a collection
of ancient Korans, ceramics, brocades, arms from the Sa-
favid dynasties. He skirted through the crowd at the museum and found himself on Chour Street next to the
mausoleum of the great mystic, Pir-i-Palandus. The delicately colored dome loomed over the narrow street and
cast its shadow upon the surging visitors. Durell turned
left this time, thought he saw the two Afghans who
worked for Chou, and turned his back to the crowd,
stopped to purchase a *yost,* a string of black prayer beads,
and two small clay tiles designed to rest the forehead
when prostrate in prayer. Nothing happened. Nobody ac-
costed him. Three minutes later he was in the street of the
silversmiths and found the shop he wanted.

The place was next to a *madressah,* a religious school,
and Durell could hear a rhythmic chanting of male voices
through the thin walls of the shop.

"I have been waiting for you, Mr. Durell," said the silversmith.

"How did you know I was coming?"

"You must not linger here. I think I am being watched.
Perhaps I shall be of no value to your people in the near
future."

"Who is watching you?"

The man shrugged. "Several men. They change posts,

and I do not know them. I think they are *ferengi*, some of them. In any case, come, have some tea; but then you must not stay longer."

"No tea, thank you. How did you know I would be here?"

"Mrs. Fingal, she is the one who told me you would soon arrive."

"Sarah Fingal?"

"Yes, sir, she is the one."

The proprietor busied himself with a small samovar set up on a plank behind his tiny smithy. The shop glittered with bangles, earrings in great hoops, silver necklaces with turquoise insets, teapots, even a silver sword. He was a thin, cadaverous man who looked as if he had worried about his health from childhood. He had a long, drooping gray moustache, thin hair, and sunken eyes that kept straying past Durell to the lane outside the tented entrance to his shop. Durell moved so that he, too, could watch the passersby. He did not see anyone who looked dangerous or even interesting.

He waited, watching the silversmith, the doorway, the narrow street beyond; he listened to the chanting of the *madressah* students, the clamor of an argument outside when a donkey blocked the street. The samovar bubbled quietly. The proprietor sipped his tea and smoothed his luxurious gray moustache.

"Sugar is very high," he murmured.

"Yes."

"The cost of everything has risen. I understand it is so even in your very rich country."

"Yes," Durell said again.

"Would you like to know where to find Sarah Fingal? She waits for you."

Durell took out his Iranian rial currency and peeled off several bills and placed them on the glass countertop above the dim and dusty silver jewelry.

"You do not expect to work for us again, is that it?" he asked.

"No, sir."

"Are you frightened?"

"I do not wish to be harmed over a matter that does not truly concern me."

"But you have been paid for information before. You have been paid well to relay information to Mr. Fingal."

"And to his Jewish wife, Mrs. Fingal," the silversmith murmured. "Is it true, as they say, that it was he who took her name when he married her, and not the other way?"

"Yes, it is true."

"A strange thing, is it not?"

"It depends on your point of view," Durell said flatly. He stared at the silversmith and waited for the inevitable.

"Fingal," the man said. "It is not a Hebrew name."

"It's Irish," Durell told him. "I understand that her father was Irish."

"Oh, yes. Yes, I see. But is it not true that if the mother is Jewish, the child is the same?"

"Sarah is Jewish, yes," Durell said. "Does it trouble you?"

"Perhaps. Could she not be an Israeli spy?"

"No."

"Ah. You sound positive. Do you like Jews?"

"As much as I like Iranians," Durell said.

The silversmith met his flat gaze for just so long, and then dropped his eyes. His face was impassive. Two centuries ago, the man would have been a wild tribesman riding to glory in Khorasan, wearing bandoliers and pistols, behind the leadership of the great Nadir Shah.

Durell said, "How much will it cost me if you tell me where to find Mrs. Fingal?"

"I think it is too dangerous to be involved in this matter. It is one thing to report on what the people in the bazaar say and think. I do not mind. I am not a traitor, I think it is harmless to make a little extra money by selling useless information and opinions to your people. But I am sure now I am being watched. Pehaps I should be silent."

"Very well." Durell turned away. "I'll find her myself."

He walked to the shop entrance and started out through the crowds thronging the bazaar. The silversmith watched him go until he was almost out of the place, and then called quietly, "Sir? Wait, please."

Durell turned but did not reenter the shop. He made himself look impatient. The silversmith came forward toward him, suddenly smiling.

"For this matter, and because I think you will now recommend that I do no more reporting for your people, I must have five thousand rials."

"Too much," Durell said.

"Five thousand, sir. Nothing less."

Durell went through the formalities of bargaining with a sense of distaste. Bargaining was necessary. Finally he learned what he needed to know. Unless the man was lying. Unless the silversmith had been bought, either by the Chinese or the Soviets. Unless he was being directed into a trap.

10

The apartment was in a small building the color of sandstone, near the park on Khwajerabi Avenue, in the northeast quadrant of the city between the park and the railroad station. It was an area of modest homes and narrow lanes, and the houses facing the street showed only blank courtyard walls with small doors recessed into the plaster. The afternoon was beginning to wane, but the accumulated heat of the day's unrelenting sun had built up within the city. Durell took a taxi to the park and walked back along Khwajerabi, threading his way through the impatient crowd, and turned off to find No. 55 Kough Road. There was a small café on the corner and an Indian store crammed with cheap general merchandise. He circled the irregular block twice, checking for vehicles, watchers, those who might be waiting here for his arrival. He saw nothing suspicious. Finally he went up a narrow stairway between two ochrous plastered walls and rapped on the blue-painted doorway, using a bronze knocker shaped in the hand of Fatima that was an emblem of good luck. It occurred to him that Homer Fingal had not had much luck at any time in his short life.

After his second rap, Sarah Fingal opened the door about two inches, recognized him, and threw back several bolts and chains to admit him. One glance at her, and he knew that she had already been informed about the death of her husband in the Seistan. She was a small, dark-haired woman with the faded blue eyes of her Irish father and the self-sufficient manner inherited from her mother. Perhaps she was a bit older than the unfortunate Homer had been. She wore a loose, elaborately embroidered Iranian robe that concealed her slight body. Her face was attractive in an intense way. Her pale eyes had violet smudges of grief smeared beneath them. Her voice was low and husky. She wore a scarf over her thick black hair, which was coiled in a tight, prim bun at the nape of her neck. The climate was too hot for that sort of thing, but her heavy hair did not seem to bother her. She touched her cheek with her left hand as she extended cool fingers for Durell's grip.

"Oh, Sam. I knew you would come. I just knew it. Did Harun tell you where to find me?"

"The silversmith? Yes. But I think you should change your address. He told me, but I think it's the end of his work for us," Durell said quietly. "I think he's been bought away from us."

"Yes, I suppose so. Did he suggest that I might be an Israeli spy?"

"Among other things," Durell paused. "I'm sorry about Homer. I got there too late. It was unavoidable, but I don't think either of us expected trouble on this."

She nodded, giving no answer to that. The tiny apartment was still littered with the evidence of Homer Fingal's scholarly research. She had been packing books in Chinese, some Sanskrit manuscripts, bric-a-brac that Homer had collected to analyze and perhaps write an academic monograph about. Cartons crammed with papers and small wooden crates stood about among the sparse Arabic furnishings in the apartment. He felt a sense of utter control about Sarah that was dangerous, leading sooner or later to an inevitable explosion of sorrow and mourning.

Sarah clasped her hands together. "Sam, I—"

"Wait." He lifted two fingers to warn her, then moved about quietly in a search of the apartment. There were two windows and a small door off the bedroom that opened onto an inner gallery. The little balcony overlooked an inside court of the building, floored with worn and faded tiles that had once formed a beautiful geometric design. A leashed dog down there looked up at him and began to bark. There was a stone outer stairway leading up from the balcony to the communal sleeping terrace on the roof. He went up quickly and quietly and looked about. No one was up here. Back in the apartment, he checked the bedroom and the bath and finally returned to the living room. The clutter prohibited anything but a cursory search for listening bugs or potential explosive devices. There was nothing he could do about the clutter, but he searched as well as he could. Sarah continued to stand motionless with her clasped hands before her. He came to her, kissed her lightly on her cold cheek, and said, "How did you learn about what happened to Homer?"

"It shows, doesn't it?"

"Of course."

"General McFee notified me. Your message to him from that village in the Seistan, via the Tehran circuit, eventually got through to Washington. Naturally, I haven't heard anything from Homer's father, as yet. I doubt if I will. The last signal came through the new jewelry shop near the INTO Tourist Bureau on Jahanbani Avenue. Do you know it?"

Durell nodded. "It was part of the briefing."

She said tightly, "But they didn't brief you or Homer about the real meaning of the assignment, did they?"

"Maybe McFee didn't know everything, then."

She turned away to the window. "Poor Homer. The perennial student. I loved him truly, Sam."

"I know."

"For once in his life, Homer tried to take an active role in today's world, instead of dwelling in the dusty past he loved so much. And it ended everything for him, past, present and future. He's dust himself now. Part of the past. Can you tell me how it happened?"

"He's dead, Sarah. Beyond pain. How it actually happened doesn't matter now."

"Do you know who did it?"

"A man who posed as an American, under the name of Mortimer Jones. He was a Russian agent, an assassin whose true name was Kokin, Leonid Kokin. I'm sure he wasn't really from the KGB, however. It's part of the things that bother me. In any case, Kokin is dead now."

"Did you kill him?"

"Yes."

"I'm glad. I believe in an eye for an eye . . ."

Sarah paused, touched her dark hair with the backward edge of her palm. Her mouth quivered briefly, and she covered it by aimlessly picking up a half-dozen books and adding them to those in one of the empty cartons. She spoke with a first touch of helplessness. "I don't know who to send these things to, Sam. I simply can't keep them."

"Send them to General Wellington, his father," Durell said.

"Him?" A world of dismay, distrust, frustration and pain welled up in her single word. "Homer's father disowned him because he married me. Because Homer wasn't strong enough to become a military man; because Homer loved books and scholarly things, not weapons and military trappings and fanfare and all the Washington scratch-my-back-and-I'll-scratch-yours political rat-race. Because Homer, as an act of rebellion, took the name of my Irish father instead of keeping his own when we married." She made a sad mouth. "A modern thing. One of the few modern things Homer ever did. He never really lived in today's world, you see. But we were in love. We loved each other. We were happy." She paused again, this time for a longer interval. "Let me get you some tea, Sam."

"Wait," he said.

He checked the stove, the gas line, and the burners. She paused with the lighted wooden match in her fingers, until he straightened and nodded and said, "Go ahead."

"You're very careful, aren't you?"

"I have to be."

"Homer wasn't careful enough, was he?"

"Homer wasn't trained for this business."

"But nobody is interested in me, Sam. I'm really quite harmless. Like Homer."

"Not any more," Durell said. "Somebody might think you know more than you do, Sarah. Somebody might believe you have something they want."

Her eyes were unafraid. "To hell with them."

"Just the same, be careful."

"Should I leave Meshed? Should I go back to the States?"

"No. I may need you here, until this is over."

"Can I help about Homer?"

"You might." He watched her set the tea kettle to boil over the blue gas flames. "I came here to learn if Homer knew where to contact and locate Nuri Qam, the Afghan Deputy Interior Minister. It's part of my assignment. Qam asked Washington for my help in the dragon matter. I knew Qam years ago, back at Yale. The whole thing wasn't supposed to be much of a job. Merely a small favor. It certainly was not supposed to cause Homer's death."

"Nuri Qam has some answers to give in Kabul, back in Afghanistan, because he lost Professor Berghetti and the Chinese artifacts—including the dragon—that Berghetti's archaeological team dug up on the Afghani side of the Seistan border."

"Berghetti also did some digging on the Iranian side of the lakes," Durell said.

Sarah nodded. "That was before he moved to Afghanistan to go on with his search. Berghetti doesn't matter. He was a thievish little man who tried to take the art treasures out of the country illegally. He's a fugitive now, and for all we know or care, he could be back in Rome at present."

"Or dead," Durell said.

She looked at his tall figure. "Maybe. Yes. But why do you say that?"

"Where can I find Nuri Qam?"

"He's right here in Meshed, Sam. Hiding out with his brother from the Afghani authorities. The brother lives here. He hopes you can help him when you arrive. He hopes you can find the dragon for him and recoup the mistake he made when he allowed Berghetti to escape with the rest of the national treasure."

"Tell me what's so important about the dragon."

"It's only an excuse," she said wearily. "They're making fools of us."

"Who are 'they?' "

"Idiots. Lunatics. General Wellington, for one. And you've heard of the Russian general, Goroschev? He leads the hawk faction in Moscow, those who are always pressing for a preemptive war against the Chinese. And of course there are fools in Peking who would also welcome a showdown at this time. It's always a question of supremacy in the Communist world. I know it sounds like a conspiracy to enlarge a small incident—the matter of the dragon—into a Sino-Soviet war; a conspiracy that's eagerly encouraged by elements on both sides. Do you think I'm crazy, Sam?"

Durell said, "If Wellington is in it, even if only by spurring them on from the sidelines, by using Homer and me, then he's inadvertently caused the death of his own son."

"But he won't lose much sleep over it," the girl said bitterly. "Considering how he felt about Homer."

Durell had met John Wellington several times in the man's plum-draped suite of offices in the EOB—the Executive Office Building close to the White House. He remembered the man's comfortable leather chairs, the highly polished oval conference table where Wellington spoke to McFee for the President, the efficient bar that could be rolled about, and the slide projector and flat screen built into the walnut-paneled walls. Wellington was a man who did not deny himself very much. He had come to the White House from the Pentagon, as a personal aide, perhaps for political reasons, and had made what seemed to be a permanent place for himself there. He had a broad Southwestern accent, an imposing physique with a mane of iron-gray hair. His physical aura usually dominated even the hard-boiled Washington press corps. He indulged in brandy and long, thin cigars and what seemed to be plain speaking.

He expressed his opinion often and forcefully about McFee's "spooks," all of it in derogatory terms. Durell remembered the man's heavy voice, heavy legs, polished Texas boots. The request for Durell's aid from Nuri Qam had come through Wellington. It hadn't seemed to be a major matter then. A question of good will toward the Afghanis, that was all. The only time that Wellington mentioned his son Homer, in Meshed, was to direct Durell to contact him for help in finding Mr. Qam. Even then, the man's hostility and contempt toward Homer and Sarah was only too evident.

"Maybe they'll be helpful to you, Cajun," he had said to Durell. "But to me, they're screwballs, both of 'em. I can't understand them. Why did Homer have to marry a Jewess? Of all the goddam stupid ass-bustin' career-wreckin' things to do! Then he took the woman's name, too, even if it was Irish, I just wrote him off, that's all. But maybe he can help you, Durell. You'll just have to play it by ear. Nuri Qam is scared shitless, hiding deep. He ain't much of a politician, I reckon, but you went to Yale with him and he asked for you, so off you go. There were two assassination attempts on Qam in the past month. He escaped 'em both and just vanished. Maybe Homer can locate him for you. And you go help him find that dragon and give it back to the Interior Ministry in Kabul. It's simple. It's harmless."

"Nothing is harmless," McFee said quietly.

Wellington grunted. "Dragons. People see dragons all the time, over Capitol Hill. Monsters. Dragons, breathing fire? Grabbing off nubile maidens?"

"All right," McFee had said. "The dragon is worth, at the most, about five million dollars as an antique art object. You put it to me, Wellington, that its recovery would be a gesture of goodwill toward Afghanistan. As simple as that? Nothing more? Find it and give it back to Kabul and pull Nuri Qam's chestnuts out of the fire, because he's a good pro-American Afghani in high political office. But it's a fire that Qam made by his own carelessness —allegedly—in letting Berghetti escape with it, in the first place. All right, I'll lend Durell to Nuri Qam, and he'll do the job and come home. What else is there?"

Wellington laughed, but his eyes glared with hostility. "What do you mean, what else? It's a simple—"

"Not with you. It can't be simple with you."

"You're seeing monsters yourself, McFee. That's the trouble with you spooks. You get kind of inbred, and your imagination runs away with you. Maybe it's a matter of bureaucratic survival, to blow something up and ask for bigger budgets. Not this time. It's a small matter. No big, scary hobgoblins in this one."

The kettle began to boil in the kitchen. Outside, in the small courtyard, the leashed dog began to bark at someone or something. Sarah got up and poured tea into delicate cloisonne cups. Durell watched her. Her hands were steady, but the tightness of her grief was evident in every movement she made.

She said, "I took several hours of the night decoding the signal from McFee in Washington. It was relayed by telephone from Tehran. I'm not very good at codes. Homer was best at it—after all, he translated Sanskrit and cuneiform as if he were reading a school primer. Even though it was in code, however, I could feel Mc-Fee's anger in it. About Homer's death, of course. And he doesn't want to lose you, Sam, just because we've been tricked into a situation he didn't know about, in the first place."

"Like what situation?"

"As I told you, they're making fools of us. Wellington, first. You've met him. You know about him. Proud of his military record—why not?—with General Patton in World War II. Then in Korea. Since that time, of course, my father-in-law has made a military-political career for himself. His patriotism runs out of his ears, even if it costs humanity its survival. He's hell-bent on America first even if it kills us all."

Sarah Fingal paused. She showed no emotion, but she did not drink her tea. "Wellington was at various SALT conferences, for instance, even Vladivostok, and had certain tidy meetings with his opposite numbers from the Soviet Union. Always with the hawks, like Goroschev. Always urging the preemptive strike, first to Moscow, then to Peking. Like, let's you and him fight, right? Like somebody egging on two mastiffs in a ring, while he sat by and watched them tear each other apart. That's what Wellington wants to happen. Then he thinks America will be safe. Even though we all know about their nuclear submarines offshore, and their orders to hit us, too, even if half of Asia and Europe is reduced to a radioactive wasteland. Maybe half our population would survive. The other half would be ashes. But then things would be run *right,* according to poor Homer's egomaniacal father."

Sarah paused again and listened to the dog barking outside. "General Goroschev is Wellington's opposite number in Moscow. They're in touch with each other, ostensibly on SALT business. McFee suggests in his new briefing that it's more than that. There's General Chan Wei-Wu, in Peking, too, for instance."

Durell said, "What did you do with McFee's transcript?"

"I burned it all," Sarah said. "Every scrap of the code. I'm just giving you the gist of things he believes you ought to know."

"All right. Go on, please."

"Wellington has a personal acquaintance with General Chan Wei-Wu, too. He went with the State Department delegation to Peking last October. Official state dinners, meeting the new Deputy Chairman. But once, as a matter of routine surveillance, he was recorded as having a thirteen-minute conversation alone with General Chan, during an official sightseeing visit to the Great Wall. No one in the party was closer to them than two hundred yards."

Durell's face was blank. "McFee listed all this as only a hypothesis, of course."

"Yes, Sam. But it's all tied up with the dragon. Two days ago there was a plenary session in Peking, headed by

General Chan, where he urged that the recently discovered treasure, like the art taken by the Nationalists to Taiwan, be claimed by the CPR as a national heritage. McFee has had signals that the Chinese are pressuring Afghanistan for an immediate return of the dragon—hence, Nuri Qam, who doesn't have it, or claims not to have it, is in hot water with Kabul. It's a Peking excuse, of course, or rather General Chan Wei-Wu's excuse, to create tension and a little border warfare, and perhaps seize a bit of territory, as they did with Tibet and India. But—" Sarah paused, staring at him.

"Go on," Durell said.

"McFee thinks that a splinter group in the Black House in Peking, directed by Chan, has sent a team into this area to find the dragon and confiscate it—steal it—and hold it for General Chan's disposition."

Durell nodded, said nothing, drank his tea.

Sarah Fingal went on, "The thing is, Wellington knew all this when he asked McFee to lend you to Nuri Qam. But you weren't briefed about the Chinese team here. You were sent here by Wellington just to muddy the waters and perhaps act as a decoy."

Durell seemed to be listening to something outside the apartment. "No, I wasn't briefed about it. And what about General Goroschev, Wellington's other pal?"

"He's another hawk, who'd like a preemptive strike by the USSR against the Chinese People's Republic. Any excuse will do to trigger off the tensions that exist along the Soviet-CPR border. Goroschev has sent a team of his own people—*not* the KGB, for the most part—here, too, to grab the dragon first. This man Kokin, whom you say killed Homer—must have been part of that other team."

"Yes, he was," Durell said.

"Goroschev won't make a secret of it if his agents grab the dragon first and take it to Moscow. He'll let the Chinese know deliberately that he's taken it. The Chinese won't be able to stand still for that insult, either. It's a matter of losing too much face, an excuse for Chan to escalate the military situation between China and the Soviets. And Wellington figures this can only work to

American advantage. As for you, you're not really *supposed* to find the dragon for Nuri Qam. You're only meant to lead the Russians to it. None of it will work to America's advantage, though. The whole world will lose. If the balance of power is upset, we'll find ourselves faced with an overwhelmingly hostile combination against us, and we'll become a declining, impotent nation." Sarah Fingal took a deep breath. "And that's the gist of Mc-Fee's new briefing for you. You're caught in a nutcracker, Sam, between the Chinese team and the Russian team."

Durell stood up. "First things first, Sarah. The dragon. Nuri Qam. Where do I find Mr. Qam?"

"I have his brother's address written down here somewhere." Sarah rummaged among the untidy heaps of books and manuscripts that littered the small living room. The narrow windows were turning dark with the dying day. A small electric fan in one of the windows ran erratically, pushing the warm air around. From one of the windows he could see over the roofs and the sleeping terraces to a wedge of the park beyond Khwajerabi Avenue, at the far corner of the little street. The trees looked dusty and lifeless. Traffic flowed eastward around the circle leading from Balukiaban. Sarah found the slip of paper finally in a battered old desk. "Here it is, Sam. But your Mr. Qam is a slippery customer, I gather. Naturally, the household refuses to admit he's there, and the Afghan authorities have no official status in Meshed. I'm surprised that Qam is your friend."

He smiled. "Not a friend, Sarah. It was a long time ago. Men and times do change."

"Well, he's slippery, all right. Won't you stay and have more tea? Or I have some Scotch. It's very expensive here, our one indulgence—I mean, Homer didn't drink much, but he liked the best. Some Scotch, Sam?"

"No, thank you."

She didn't want him to go. He wondered how many visitors or friends they'd had here. Not many, he supposed. The American community, small as it was, would have shunned the Fingals cruelly because of General Wellington's ostracism. He looked at her thoughtfully, and considered the bars and locks on the door and windows.

"How much food do you have in the place?" he asked.

She was puzzled. "I don't know. Enough for two or three days. Why?"

"I'd like you to stay here. Indoors. Lock yourself in, Sarah. There may be no danger for you, but you never can tell. And I need you by the telephone. I'll be calling you, and I'd like to set you up as a relay link to Tehran and Washington."

She hesitated. "I don't know if I want to go on with your business, Sam."

"I'll need your help," he said simply.

She brushed aside her hair again with the back of her hand. Her eyes remained doubtful for a few moments more, then she nodded. "All right, Sam. There were others who helped to kill Homer, weren't there?"

"Yes."

"Will you get them for me?"

"Yes."

"Very well," she agreed. "I'll stand by here."

Ten minutes later, he was gone. Before he left, he memorized the address on the scrap of paper she had given him, and then he burned the paper in an ashtray.

11

He went first to the little hotel where he had taken the room with Anya Talinova. He did not think anyone followed him from Sarah Fingal's place. He had seen no sign of Chou or Zhirnov, but he scouted the area carefully before entering the tiny hotel lobby and going up to the room. It was dusk, and the lights of the cinemas on Pahlevi Avenue began to wink and blink with their evening displays—the only nightlife permitted and sanctioned in the holy city of Meshed. The stairway to the upper floor was of stone, rising against the lobby wall on the left-hand side above an arched entrance to a *tchaikana*, a local tearoom run by the hotel. Nobody seemed to be in the restaurant.

The upper hallway was narrow and dimly lighted. The heat that had collected there felt insufferable.

At the doorway to the room he paused and listened. A radio played an Arabic Love song, crooning softly; it was the current hit from an Egyptian movie. The sound came from down the hall. Through the high-pitched radio music he heard a faint scuffling in the room, then silence, then a few light footfalls. He wasn't sure if it was a man or a woman in there. He took the key to the room in his hand, started to open the door, then paused again. He did not think it was Anya inside. He heard something splash.

98

A trickle of water was running. But he wasn't sure it was water, either.

Durell backed away, moved on down the hall, found a flight of stairs going up to the sleeping roof. Several of the hotel's guests had already put mattresses and netting on the terrace, in preparation for the warm night. They looked at him curiously as he moved past them to the edge of the roof overlooking his room window. A faint light came through the dusty glass panes below. The radio now was bellowing propaganda from the room next door, the guttural Arabic words almost hysterical, importunate and triumphant at the same time. There was a rickety wooden stairway, applied as an afterthought, attached to the back wall. He went down one flight to his room level, ignoring the curious stares of those on the sleeping terrace, and found he could reach the tiny ornamental balcony outside the window, if he could swing across just right from the wooden steps. The night was full of sounds now. He didn't know if the ornamental balcony would hold his weight or not; he hoped so.

He leaped lightly from the steps to the balcony, caught the railing, swung precariously over the back alley, heard the flimsy metal creak, thought he was going to fall, then pulled himself up, caught a toehold on the narrow ledge, drew himself further up, and rested, flat against the wall of the hotel beside the window.

He breathed lightly, listening.

A woman was humming, inside his room.

It was not Anya.

The voice was deeper, more full-chested, and then he caught a murmured German word or two. He crouched on the ledge, saw that the lower sash of the window was open, although the flimsy curtain was drawn beyond it.

He dived through, tearing the curtain, hit the grimy rug on the floor, and rolled over. He came up with the gun in his hand pointed at the tall woman who stood at the wash basin and tin tub in the corner, opposite the bed.

It was Freyda Hauptman-Graz.

She had taken the opportunity, while obviously waiting for him, to strip and use the facilities to wash the travel grime from her tall, voluptuous body, and she stood looking at him with only mild surprise on her face. She clutched a thin towel in front of her. Her legs looked long and powerful. The thin, small towel was entirely inadequate.

"Please," she whispered. "No noise. No guns. Do not speak my name."

"Don't move," he said.

"Whatever you say."

The tall Nordic woman was outlined against the winking, blinking cinema lights that came through the other window. She did not look in the least frightened. He glanced about the room in the dim light for traces of Anya. The Russian girl was gone. It was as if she had never been here. He looked at his watch and saw that he had left her for more than the two hours she had promised to stay. He had told her to wait that long, and he hadn't expected her to wait any longer, but—

"Where is she?" he asked softly.

"You speak of the Russian girl? But no one was here, when I came in," said Freyda.

"Wasn't the door locked?"

"No, it was open. I was a little surprised about that, myself."

"Don't lie to me."

"I did not come here for that. I came to make a deal, a business proposition, and while I waited here for you, I made myself comfortable. Do you mind?"

Her clothes, shoes, skirt and blouse, were tossed in a heap on the bed. Her purse, of fine cream-colored leather, was open amid her pile of clothing. He moved to it, dumped out the contents, saw tiny Parisian perfume bottles and lipstick and passport and a ring of keys. No weapons. She had used some of the perfume on herself while she waited, and the scent was too strong, too overwhelming, no more subtle than she was. She watched him with amusement kindled in her pale gray eyes. She was not as young as he had thought, when he met her first on the plane and later, during the episode in the bazaar. She was careless about the skimpy towel that covered her from breasts to hips.

"What kind of a deal?" he asked.

"My husband Hans, you met him, of course, he is in the local hospital. He is very painfully wounded, so he is now out of it. Mr. Chou and his other people are looking for you everywhere in the city, did you know that?"

He nodded and waited.

"I took my husband's wallet, and so I have all his money and am independent of him now. I do not care about him. Let Mr. Chou take care of all the expenses. It does not matter to me. I never wanted to get mixed up in this affair, anyway."

"So?"

She smiled. Her eyes invited him to remove the towel. "May we make a deal, perhaps?"

"For what?"

"The dragon, of course, May I buy it from you?"

"I don't have it," Durell said.

"Ah, *bitte*—"

"Do you want the dragon for yourself?"

"I understand that as an object of art, it is truly worth a fortune. Perhaps as much, perhaps more than five or six of your million dollars. It is no good to you for that, I suppose, even if you could find the proper market. You would not be interested in the dragon for that, would you? For yourself, *Herr* Durell?"

"No," he said shortly.

"I did not think so. You are a man of—business ethics? Proud of your profession? But, you see, I am sick of this shadow-world life. I want—how do you say it?—I want to get out. For myself, alone. Privately. Most personally. But in comfort, do you understand? With what I feel is owed to me. I have lived in this—this gray world— much too long. I have had to do things that I despise myself for. Ah, but if I had the dragon! Ah! Then I could take it to South America—I do not care if you know about this—where there are some of the Old Guard still living, the Gestapo villains, they made a good life for themselves there. My father—you needn't know about him—had dossiers, bank records, shipping accounts—everything about them. They could help me, they would *have* to help me, I could hang them. I could make a bargain with the collectors, perhaps even hold a private auction. And I could retire and live far away from Berlin—"

"You come from *East* Berlin," he corrected her.

"Yes. East, West, I could get away from it all. I am sick to my soul of it. I am frightened by it. In our business, dear Cajun, once the fear gets in your blood, it is like cancer, eh? It weakens you and you die. I want the dragon. I need it. I must have it. I wish to buy it from you. Please, please accommodate me. I am desperate."

She did not look or sound very desperate. But perhaps she was telling the truth—partially—about herself. She had within her the air of a predator that Durell had seen before in men and women involved in his business. It would always be Freyda first, with her; and the devil take the hindmost. He watched her move, her figure rich and magnificent behind the thin gray towel. Her legs were long and full-fleshed, her buttocks plump, her waist very narrow; she held the towel so that her arm pushed her provocative breasts up to where they were deliberately revealed, exhibiting their own interest in him.

The cinema lights in the window behind her blinked on and off. Obviously, she could not be carrying a concealed weapon. Not the usual type, he thought wryly. But she could have planted a gun, a bomb, a knife, somewhere in the room, in the time she had been alone in here. He wondered if she had done something to Anya, removing her forcibly somewhere else, in order to take her place. But the room did not reflect any violence, only the sadness of past clientele. He listened to the muffled noises from the other rooms in the hotel, and considered exits and entrances—the narrow corridor, the rickety wooden steps in the rear, the stairway that came up over the restaurant from the street lobby.

Freyda said impatiently, "Are you listening to me?"

"Yes."

"You do not look at me very much."

"I see you," Durell said.

"Do you not like what you see?"

"Yes."

"Listen," she said imperatively. "How long have you been in this business, Cajun? I've heard so much about you before this—oh, yes, we have our dossiers on you, too. I have always wondered if you were like the talented and dangerous man described in the read-outs. And you turn out to be more so." She made her voice softer. "Always, although I was married to a poor excuse of a husband, I wondered how I would feel and what I would do, if I met a man like you."

"You're being obvious, Freyda," he said. He looked at the outline of her body through the thin towel. "In more ways than one."

"What would it take to buy the dragon from you?" she whispered. And then she came closer. "How much money?"

"Not enough in the world," he said. "And I don't have it, anyway."

"But you know where the dragon is," she insisted.

"Maybe," he admitted. "Maybe I do, now."

"Would a new world of safety and freedom—and me?—be attractive to you, then? Surely you are tired of hunting and being hunted. One never grows old in this business. One dies, suddenly, usually very badly. There is no retirement for people like you and me. Unless we escape, somehow. Into anonymity, yes? With money. Lots of money. New names, new identity, new papers. And then the freedom to be one's true self, without constant fear of every shadow."

Now she was within touching distance of him, and he scented her perfume, and knew she had been liberal with it, all over that magnificent body. She looked sidelong at the bed. "We are safe here, for the moment. It is quiet here. I was lucky, just lucky, to see Anya leaving this hotel as I was passing by. That is how I found you. I was discreet coming up here. No one, certainly not Mr. Chou, knows I am here with you."

She put her arms up and locked her hands behind his

neck. He did not like it. She could easily develop it into a paralyzing, spine-breaking grip. She was big enough and strong enough. The towel fell to the floor in a heap between them. Her breasts pressed against his chest, firm and goddesslike. He laughed softly, moved forward, kissed her. She changed at once, sensing a victory, and pulled him toward the bed. Her mouth was anxious, eager, ripe and demanding. When they were up against the bed, he murmured softly against her open mouth, "To hell with you, Freyda."

Her anger flashed like an eruptive volcano. She was as strong as he had suspected, and more. Her training was good. She tried to pull his head forward, to smash his face against the top of her head, but he was ready for her, and dropped out of her locked hands behind his neck, got his shoulder into her ribs, and heaved her backward upon the sagging bed. She made a small sound of dismay, bounced, her legs flying up to kick him low in the belly, missing her major target. Her thick blond hair came awry out of its neat, tight coils. Naked, she looked up at him with a face darkened by fury.

"Oh, you bastard—"

"Take it easy, Freyda. It's just no deal."

"I could have turned you over to Chou—"

"Perhaps you should have."

He was right about her having stashed a weapon in the little hotel room. Her hand slid under the dingy pillow and came up with a six-inch blade, razor-sharp, honed to a point as thin as a needle. She drove it at him and he slid aside, caught for her wrist, missed, felt a thin hissing pain in his upper arm, then captured her wrist and twisted, came down with all his weight upon her. She was all woman, all fury, all murder. She thrust upward under him, trying to free her knife hand, and he came down harder, felt her teeth sink into the side of his neck. He hit her with his left fist, hit her again as she pulled up a knee into his groin. She yelped, groaned, slid aside, yielding the knife, and fell off the bed on the opposite side. He saw the flash of her long, firm thighs and hips and buttocks as she sprawled on the dusty floor. Her long blond hair flew wildly. He caught at a heavy braid, wrapped it around his hand, and tugged her head back hard. She got to her knees, her strength that of a man's, her efforts practiced and expert. Durell put a foot against her quivering buttocks and shoved hard. She sprawled forward with a cry of outrage.

Smoothly, he dropped a knee on her back and used his hand on the nape of her neck to press her face against the grimy little rug. She heaved and struggled, her naked body writhing. He pressed his weight down harder until she suddenly groaned and began cursing softly in German.

"Now we'll have the truth," he said softly.

"Oh, you are cruel—!"

"The truth," he repeated.

"I have told you all—more than I ever told anyone else—"

"But not enough," he said.

"Please—let me up."

He pressed down harder. She groaned again, tried to reach back and claw up his flexed knee that pressed into the firm flesh of her rump.

"Freyda, be very careful. Be very quiet. It won't do either of us any good if you raise an alarm and get the police up here. The local jail isn't any bed of roses."

"Yes, yes . . ." she gasped. "Let me at least turn over. My breasts hurt—they are crushed on the floor—"

He released his weight carefully and she rolled over on one ample hip, then onto her back. Her long legs came up slowly on either side of him. Her eyes were blind with fury. There were red splotches on her cheek where he had forced her face into the rough, dirty rug. Her chest heaved, her breasts moving upward. He forced himself to pay no attention.

He said quietly, "You have good reason for deserting your husband and Mr. Chou. You know how dangerous that can be, however. The Black House would never let you live a single day, a single hour, with any peace of mind." His voice was low and persuasive. "You know how it is in our business. You're an intelligent woman.

What you told me about wanting to pull out of the business, with the dragon, and live in South America, was all lies. You have other reasons."

"No, no," she whispered. "I swear it—"

She tried to wrap her long legs around him as he straddled her. Durell dropped a forearm across her throat and pressed his weight down hard again. She couldn't breathe. Her face turned purple, ugly with hatred and terror. When her eyes started to roll, he released his weight on her windpipe. She drew her breath in with a long, rasping, rattly hiss. He waited until some of the purple color faded.

"Everybody is afraid of the Black House people," he said gently, looking down at the big woman. "Anybody with any sense, that is. So I figure you have a bigger fear, something you're more afraid of than Peking's vengeance if you betray them. What is it, Freyda?"

"Nothing."

"What is it?"

"Nothing."

He applied pressure again. His face was blank, without expression, as he hurt her. This time her ripe body flopped, bucked, and bounced under him, between his legs. It took her longer to recover, when he at last relented.

"Well?"

"My sister—"

"Who?"

"Wilma Strelsky. Madame Strelsky. The mistress of General Chan Wei-Wu."

"In Peking?"

"Yes. Oh, yes. She is in Peking. She wants a visa to Hong Kong, official papers, so she can escape and come home. It is not given to her. General Chan keeps her there, in the city, in Peking, just as a prisoner for his pleasure. He will not release her."

"We're talking about the same General Chan who sent the Chinese team—you and your husband and I suppose others—in here for the dragon?"

"Yes. Yes, of course. The man who wants war. The

man everyone on the Committee is so terribly afraid of. Except for the Deputy Chairman. He stands out. The Deputy Chairman is General Chan's enemy. It is no secret. The Deputy Chairman understands the folly of nuclear war."

"How do you know this?"

"My sister and I—Wilma and I—we have secret correspondence. It is in a childhood code. It is so simple, so obvious, it is not suspected. She writes to me."

"And what does she write that makes you want to double-cross the Chinese—General Chan's—team?"

"Wilma is part of a plot. The Deputy Chairman is using her, too. He has offered her a release from China, an escape from General Chan's attentions and imprisonment. She does not want to be Chan's mistress forever, or until she is old and then discarded and made to work in the fields, or in some factory commune making bicycle parts. She is truly a prisoner there, you see—unofficial, uncounted, with no one to speak for her or even aware of her. And only the Deputy Chairman can save her."

"How?" Durell asked harshly.

"I do not know the politics of the inner ruling circles in Peking, but—"

She was reluctant to go on. He waited, patient and watchful, his blue eyes very dark. He wondered about Wilma's existence in the unlikely lovenest in distant Peking. Freyda's breath was still ragged.

"They will kill General Chan Wei-Wu," Freyda went on slowly. "Wilma is part of the plan. She will keep Chan with her, in her apartment, so Chan's personal guards can be quietly eliminated, and then they will come in and kill Chan. It is the Deputy Chairman's idea. This new Deputy is against using the dragon as an excuse for war. He is sensible, secretly a scholar in the old tradition, Wilma says. He is a great admirer of the ancient scholar-artist, Tung Ch'i-ch'ang. The Deputy is a subtle man. It will look like suicide, on the part of the General. Wilma will be hurried out of the country and given to Hong Kong as a reward for her cooperation, and she will be safe. So Mr. Chou, from the Black House, will have no further business here in Meshed, when he learns that the General is dead. It will all be over. No more orders to Chou from the General. But I do not want to go on with the business. I do not wish to go on living like this. I want the dragon. For myself and for Wilma, who has suffered enough."

Durell felt a weariness that was not betrayed in the lines of his face. Cross and double cross, and motives within motives. It was almost standard, something always to be expected in this business.

"When will the General be executed?" he asked.

"Tonight or tomorrow. Perhaps it has happened already," Freyda said. She seemed more confident now. She looked down at her body as she lay sprawled beneath him and held her bruised breasts in both hands. Somehow, even now, the gesture was provocative. She said, "I mentioned the ancient artist, Tung, whom the Deputy Chairman admires?"

"He was a man who used brush and ink, shortly after the school of color painting flourished in the T'ang dynasty," Durell said.

She was pleased. "*Ach,* yes. You know of him! Tung was a *wen-jen,* a true gentleman-scholar. He did not believe in debating with himself over each movement of his brush; the art of painting in his day came from the heart, the spirit. Therefore it was mostly truthful and serene. Tung was a master of all the strokes of the brush, from the lute string to the twenty-one *ts'un,* the wrinkled texture, as it was called. He had the vital rhythm, the *ch'i-yün;* he captured the *ch'i,* the spirit of his subjects, to a delicate perfection. You see, the Deputy Chairman is an artist like Tung Ch'i-ch'ang. It is important to know such things about a man. He will be successful. The murder of the General, to end the Dragon plot, will come off to a perfection equal to Tung's art. Then Wilma will be free to leave China. And Mr. Chou, from the Black House, will find himself at a loss here in Meshed, with no purpose, no mission, no superior to give him orders, and no reason to pursue the dragon further. Do you understand now, Durell? All the effort of the Chinese team, of which I am a part—or was—will go for nothing. It will all be erased, cancelled. Without the General, the Russians cannot provoke war. So the dragon is up for—how do you say it?—up for grabs."

He wondered if she was stalling for time. He had not needed the lecture on ancient Chinese artists. He had let Freyda go on with it, pondering the irony of what might be happening thousands of miles away in Peking, if she were telling the truth. And he considered how it affected his own assignment.

"Bitte," she said. "Please. I have told you the whole truth now. Let me up. Please.'

He released his weight on her warm body and got to his feet. The woman flexed her knees, rolled over, rested for a moment on all fours. She faced away from him. She did not seem to be conscious of her nudity. When she finally stood up, she leaned against a small, battered table in the corner that was part of the room's primitive furnishings. Her hip went askew.

"Then you will help me, Cajun? I have been utterly honest with you. Can I somehow buy the dragon from you? I have not too much money of course, but I have much information you can use, on networks and post office drops and radio relays. Oh, much, much data. Better still if you would join with me. We can share the profits. We can—"

"No."

"You truly do not have the dragon?"

"Put your clothes on, Freyda."

"You are not much of a man, after all," she sneered.

Then, all at once, she made her move. He had been right about her having concealed a weapon in the room, the knife with which she had first attacked him on the bed, but he had not given her credit for arranging another backstop. With surprising speed for such a large woman, she opened the drawer in the small table she leaned against and snatched up a small, nickel-plated .28 pistol she had hidden there. Crouching, she fired at him twice, holding the gun in both hands. Her face was contorted by hatred.

The first slug went through the single window with a

shattering crash of broken glass. The second bullet whipped past Durell's throat with a hot, burning sensation. He gave her no time for a third effort. He dived hard at her, careless of the noise now, after the reckless shots she had fired. The whole hotel and neighborhood would be alerted and alarmed in minutes. He slammed her hard against the wall, saw the icy fury in her eyes, and hit her with his fist, saw blood spurt from her mouth, hit her again, caught the little pistol as she dropped it, and let her fall without ceremony to the floor in a naked heap.

He took a deep breath, straightened, and found that he was trembling.

Somebody shouted from the floor below. A piece of glass fell belatedly from the window frame. The garish movie lights on Pahlevi Avenue winked on and off.

Turning, he opened the hotel room door with caution. The narrow, dimly lighted corridor was still deserted, but footsteps thudded upward from the lobby. He turned to the right, moved down the back steps. Each tread creaked an alarm as he ran lightly downward to the alley entrance. He already heard the far-off hooting of a police siren.

People were craning over the edges of their roof terraces as he reached the alley floor. The smells here were noisome. A cat squealed and leaped away. Dogs barked. Lights were going on everywhere.

He ran to the end of the alley, came out on the street, turned left, walked two blocks north into a better lighted avenue. A bus came rumbling along. He put up his hand and boarded it and rode away.

12

The neighborhood was one of imposing villas, some in European style, most in the hidden Moslem design of a high surrounding wall enclosing an inner courtyard. Heavily leafed trees made pools of quiet shadow from which he moved toward the single door in the wall facing the street. The house bulked high beyond the wall, with terraced roofs, some with planted gardens. A fountain tinkled somewhere within the grounds. Durell lifted the traditional hand of Fatima as a door-knocker and rapped twice, then twice again. It was only nine o'clock in the evening.

He waited.

He stood close against the wall beside the door and watched the street. No vehicles. No pedestrians. They were far from the center of town, northwest on the road going to Qushan. Beyond the little suburb stretched flat fields of fruit orchards and vegetables. The moon rode high in a hot, clear sky. Low hills, rising to an occasional high peak, lay to the east and west, and atop the peaks here and there were the dim outlines of ancient ruined fortresses dating far back to the devastating Uzbek invasions of the area.

He knocked again.

This time he heard bolts withdrawn, a small bell tinkled, and a voice asked in Farsi what he wanted at this hour.

"Mr. E.K. Qam, please."

"Not here, sir."

"His brother, then. Mr. Nuri Qam."

"Never heard of him, sir."

"Tell him it's Durell," he said quietly.

"Durell?"

"Hurry."

"Wait, please."

The bolts were shot home again. It seemed like a long wait before the door was opened again and he was finally admitted. Two large Afghanis in tribal costumes stood to either side of him. They were armed with snubby-barreled automatic rifles slung over their shoulders.

"This way, Mr. Durell. Please be as quiet as possible. Mr. Qam does not wish to disturb the ladies, who are asleep on the roof."

"Thank you."

One of the men said respectfully. "You speak very good Farsi, sir."

"Pashto, and Dari, too," Durell said.

"Allah has blessed you. Come, please. Mr. Qam has been awaiting your arrival for several days."

There was an inner court where a fountain played over a blue-tiled mosaic basin the size of a small swimming pool. Feathery trees grew up against the fretwork galleries of the second floor, and he heard the sleepy twitter of caged birds somewhere. The moonlight was bright enough to let him see everything quite clearly. None of the rooms on the lower floor were lighted, but as they crossed the inner courtyard a light bloomed up above, on a second-level terrace reached by a stone stairway that hugged a blank wall. A voice called softly and one of the Afghani tribesmen answered in a reassuring tone. The place was like a fortress, Durell thought; once within the gates, it revealed another world, private and secret, armed against intruders. Nuri Qam's brother, who had offered Nuri sanctuary here against the hostility of official Kabul, was evidently a man of considerable wealth. In the gardens were relics of the antique past, bulbous serpentine columns and pieces of time-worn statuary. The scent of spices and aromatic flavors drifted on the quiet night air.

"Sam? Samuel? Is that you? Praise Allah, you got here at last."

Nuri Qam came out of the shadows of the second-level terrace and beckoned him upward. In an altered voice, querulous and arbitrary, Nuri Qam dismissed the two genial guards.

"Sam, Sam. Have you eaten? Have you had dinner?"

"Not yet."

"I shall order something from the kitchens. A real Afghan meal; you will enjoy it, I promise you, and we will talk while you eat, yes?"

Nuri Qam had changed since their university days together. In New Haven, Nuri was a thin, intense youth preoccupied with the future of his troubled, backward country. He had been religious and abstemious, of complete morality, and he ignored the normal undergraduate frolics. But now apparently some inherited wealth and the soft life of upper officialdom had worked its way with him. It was difficult for Durell to see the slender, dedicated youth in this gross, overblown, softly rounded man. Qam wore a full white silk embroidered blouse and loose trousers of dark material stuffed into soft boots. His fat hands were ornamented with too many rings, and he had grown bald except for a fringe of dark hair around his shining scalp. He carried a prayer book in his left hand as he wrung Durell's fingers. His belly forbade the traditional hug and kiss, for which Durell was grateful. Qam's face, round as the moon sailing in the night sky, was jowly and wreathed in smiles. But the moonlight revealed an inner caution, a reserve, perhaps, that echoed the hunted man as he surveyed Durell's height.

"Good, good. I needed you, I sent for you, and here you are. Difficult to believe! Ever since our days at Yale, I have admired the good old U.S.A. I am in terrible difficulties, Sam, terrible. It is so good of your agency to lend you to me in this most embarrassing and awkward situation. And dangerous. Yes, I cannot stress that too much.

Dangerous." Nuri Qam paused, his hand at Durell's elbow, and looked up at him sharply. "You understand, you have been lent to me, to be employed only by me? That you work strictly for me?"

"That was the assignment."

"Excellent, excellent. We shall get along very well in resolving this terribly urgent matter."

"You're talking about the dragon?"

"Of course. What else? It has preyed on my mind ever since that foolish little archaeologist, Professor Berghetti, tried to smuggle it out of Afghanistan."

"And where is Berghetti now?"

"Later. Later, we shall talk. First you must eat, yes?" Nuri Qam clapped his ringed hands, and a stout, veiled woman appeared, to whom he gave rapid orders in Dari. Then Qam led Durell into the building, through a modified Moorish archway. The entire household was either asleep or moving about on terrified tiptoe, Durell reflected.

Twenty minutes later he was seated crosslegged on a cushion upon the floor, before a dark red embroidered cloth spread upon the Khorasan rug, being served a hot meal. He ate without reserve, feeling a sudden enormous hunger. The stout, veiled woman, who might have been Qam's wife or merely the household cook, brought him *maushawa,* a soup that included beans and meatballs and tomato sauce, then *shashlik.* The triple squares of mutton were juicy and tender on the *sir,* the skewer, alternated with wedges of fat from the sheep's tail. Dish after dish appeared, yoghurt marinades of garlic and vinegar, more grilled kebabs with *pilaus* spiced with coriander and pepper, cardamom and cloves, topped with raisins and chopped nuts. He was served an Iranian wine in a tall goblet crusted with gold; very strong *chai sia,* black tea in scalding hot cups; and of course sweets of all sorts, figs and fruit and small rice cakes called *kolchas.* There were no utensils, and he used only the crusty *nan,* flat bread, to scoop up the food. Nuri Qam smiled continuously and did not join him until the desserts arrived, whereupon he reached across the cloth-covered rug and ate greedy handsful.

During the meal, Qam insisted on talking of nothing but his years in the States, his education, his brother who had gone to Cambridge and then emigrated to Iran, where his business had prospered enormously. The brother, Qam said, was presently in Tehran closing a deal. Qam did not identify the nature of the business or the deal, but Durell, surveying the long narrow room, with its masonry fretwork opening onto the long balcony, the opulent furnishings and the art objects, did not question his host about it. He noted, however, several fine European paintings, a French inlaid cabinet of rosewood and Cellini gold, along with antique objects from the Sassanid and the Seljuk dynasties prior to the tidal wave of armies led by Togrul Beg a millenium ago. There were fine gold-handled swords, round Mongol shields, an illuminated Koran, double the size of an average book. There were Turkoman robes and rugs, Uzbek helmets, all ranged around the high-ceilinged room which was decorated with tiles and mosaics inscribed with flowing Arabic script in gilt letters against blue.

"Your brother is an art collector?" Durell finally asked.

"Of sorts, of sorts." Nuri Qam waved a disparaging hand. "You see here only a small part of his collections. He can grow very passionate one moment, and neglect it all the next. It is not of our concern."

"The thought occurs to me," said Durell, "that perhaps he would like what we call the Afghan Dragon added to his private collection."

"Yes, I realized the thought would occur to you, Sam. But you must put it from your mind at once. It is an intolerable idea. Truly, we must not begin with mistrust."

"That's how I survive in my business," Durell said.

"But then," Nuri smiled, "why would I have sent for you, a man of your reputation and esteem, a man who is feared by both Russian and Chinese alike? Yes, your capacities, your professional abilities, are well known to me. I never forgot about you, you see. I have followed your career with the utmost interest. And of all the men in the world, I have turned to you."

"To recover the dragon," Durell said flatly.

"Yes. Naturally."

"For whom?" he asked quietly.

Nuri Qam's dark eyes were subtle. "For my government, naturally. It is ours."

"Is it worth the threat of an invasion?"

"We have our pride."

"Will Kabul give it back to the Chinese People's Republic, who claim the dragon?"

"Never." Nuri was emphatic. "It is a matter of national honor. We will not be bullied over it. We are quite without fear, whatever private threats Peking makes."

"And the Soviets? Where do they come into it?"

"They would merely like to embarrass Peking by gaining possession of the dragon. This is a matter that does not concern me."

"It concerns me," Durell said, thinking of Fingal. "Why are you hiding here, Nuri, in this place, which is like a fortress?"

"I fear for my life, and the lives of my wives and children. They are all sheltered here. Certain political enemies would like me removed because I made several embarrassing mistakes in this matter." Nuri struggled to his feet, his ponderous weight getting in his way. "Come. We shall talk upstairs."

"This room is good enough," Durell said. He remained seated. "You want me to find the dragon?"

"Of course. Why else—?"

"But I think you have it already, Nuri," Durell said.

13

Nuri Qam looked at Durell as if he were lost in a sudden dream. Durell rose softly to his feet.

"How long have you been in Meshed, Sam?" Nuri asked vacantly.

"Since noon."

"Nine hours, then."

"Yes, nine hours."

"And here, in this country?"

"Almost two days."

"Two days. And I sent for you four days ago?"

"So I was told."

"Yes, on Monday. And in so short a time, you have come to the conclusion that *I*, who sent for you to find it, have the dragon?"

"Yes."

"Why?"

"The Russians don't have it; they're killing for it. They killed the contact man, Homer Fingal; did you know that, Nuri?"

"No, I was not told."

"The Chinese don't have it, either; they're looking for it and they're ready to kill for it, too. They have two Afghanis as muscle men and a Chinese controller, a Mr. Chou. Ever heard of him?"

"No, I—"

"There is also a German couple working for the Chinese, right?"

"I don't know about them, either."

"And Berghetti has vanished. Tell me about Professor Berghetti," Durell suggested.

Nuri Qam spoke as if to the warm night air blowing in through the Moorish arches around the terrace. "I was afraid of leaks. I was afraid of someone else learning about it. Berghetti was foolish, but he did not talk, except to me. Yet it reached the newspapers and the world; it went to Peking and Moscow. I was appalled. But these things do happen. There are always ears that listen, tongues that wag. So I was afraid. I do not want to die yet, although the time will come when Allah calls for me, and I will have to go. But I enjoy life. There is time enough for Paradise, eh?"

"Berghetti," Durell reminded him.

"He was put in custody, on my orders, in Herat, across the border. I went from Kabul to interview him. I was coming this way, anyway, to visit my brother here and his family. Berghetti finally showed me the dragon. He was very contrite. He admitted he had made a foolish mistake, trying to smuggle it out of Afghanistan."

"You actually saw the dragon? It exists?"

"Oh, yes. On my word. It is real enough."

"And what happened to Berghetti?"

"I gave him his parole. You must understand—" Nuri Qam paused and swallowed and spread his fat hands. The jeweled rings flashed in the light. "I was fascinated. I share my brother's love for antiquities, for the beauties of the past, for jewels and fine art objects. It is a passion with me, not as much as it is with my brother, but a passion, nonetheless. I talked for hours with Berghetti, after he told me where he had hidden the dragon and I saw it. We talked about his digs and what he found and where. We—I thought we were friends. I was prepared to advocate leniency for his attempt to smuggle the treasure out of Afghanistan. It was a mistake. He betrayed me. He escaped and took back the dragon, which I was holding personally in my possession."

"And no word from him since?"

"Oh, yes. He tried to make his way to Pakistan, through Qali-i-Kang, in the Afghan Seistan, where he made his find originally. Then he went by road to Farahrod and Ghirisk toward the eastern border. A foolish man, as I said. He is still in that region. Privately jailed. With the rest of his treasures made secure. None of his other finds were as important as the dragon, of course, but still—of great value. Yes, great value." Qam all but smacked his lips. "He can rot there in that provincial jail, for all I care."

"But you kept the dragon. He didn't really get it back from you, did he?" Durell said.

"Yes. The Chinese want it. Kabul wants it, of course. The Soviets want it just to stir up trouble. And I want it, too, of course."

Durell said, "Where is it, Nuri?"

"Here. In this room. Just over there."

Durell moved quietly across the long, narrow chamber, aware of the beautiful ornamentation that surrounded him; he felt as if he were in some palace of the Caliph Harun el-Raschid, of bygone days. In the year 817 Ali Reza had died after asking to be buried next to the Caliph of Baghdad, his archenemy, as a sign of vindication and rebuke. Those were the days and nights of bloody daggers and subtle poisons, Durell thought. He watched the stout figure of Nuri Qam from a corner of his eye, never letting the man out of his sight.

The box was small, about twelve inches square and nine inches deep. It was crusted with pearls and ornate gold, with gilded hasps for the lid and inlaid mother-of-pearl again set in script from the Koran. In itself, the box was a treasure. It was relatively new, however, and obviously had not lain buried in the Afghan deserts for a thousand years before Professor Berghetti and his crew of hippie workers dug it up. Durell lifted the box gently and was surprised by its weight.

"There is no keyhole," he said.

"And no key," said Nuri Qam.

"Open it."

"It's a secret."

"I want to see the dragon, Nuri. This was supposed to be a simple search and delivery job. I want to see what I'm supposed to deliver. Open it, Nuri."

"Very well, Sam."

Durell wondered if Nuri Qam had a weapon under his loose blouse or in the baggy trousers tucked into his soft boots. The Afghani took the box from him and held it in a certain way, turning its narrow end toward him; he pressed it against his bulging belly, his fingers moving over the inlay of nacre, and there came a small, well-oiled click. The lid sprang up.

Durell did not take the box from Nuri Qam's hands.

"Lift it out," he said.

"So. You do not trust me, Sam?"

"You still have some things to explain."

"In good time, old friend. Yes, all will be made clear. So here is the dragon, this thing that nations will quarrel over and threaten dreadful war. A thing of beauty, but not so beautiful as to warrant the death of millions. Merely an excuse for war. A spur to the showdown between our monstrous neighbors to the north, eh? Here. The dragon."

Even in Durell's eyes, he knew he was looking at something of exquisite, classical beauty.

There was something of the T'ang style in the translucent jade body of the dragon, in the manner in which the vicious little head was raised, the way the ruby eyes glared with a malevolence a thousand years old. Between its golden fangs, cunningly locked within the jaws, was a large, gleaming pearl. The tiny back was tipped with gold, as were the upraised claws. The projecting tongue was another exquisitely shaped ruby. But the intrinsic value of the statuette had nothing to do with the price it might command in the world's art market. Five million was a low estimate of its price. It felt extraordinarily heavy in his hands.

"The belly," Nuri Qam said softly. His dark eyes gleamed with passion. "It carries in its belly an egg of solid gold."

It did, indeed. Durell stared at it for a moment more, then lifted it and returned it to its carved box. Nuri Qam snapped the lid shut with a small click.

"Let him stay in darkness for a little longer," Qam murmured. "He did not mind waiting for ten centuries. He was a secret appeal, you know, from Prince Chan to the local rulers; a bribe to resist the Mongol hordes. An appeal for war and massacre, to turn the Hamun lakes red with blood. And so it happened. But it was the Mongols who made their mountains of skulls from the heads of their enemies. And the dragon slept until now."

Durell said, "He could awaken new monsters to ravage the world."

"Yes, he could."

"So you had it all along?"

"Yes."

"To keep for yourself?"

"I fled from Herat with it, across the border, to this sanctuary." Nuri Qam's voice trembled slightly now. "I was in fear of my life. I still am. I could appeal to no one. Not even my government would help me. It was—how would you say it, so inelegantly—a hot potato. Only if I can appear in Kabul with it can I reinstate myself against the wishes of my political enemies. And I cannot take it there myself. Someone—deliberately, I am sure—has been threatening the airlines with bombs, kidnapping, skyjacking. So security is very tight. If I carried the dragon into the airport to board a plane, it would be discovered in the routine of special search now going on among the passengers. I do not want that to happen. I doubt if I could even reach the airport alive, eh? But you came here, Sam, all the way from the States. You are here now. I begin to believe you can do anything. You can take the dragon for me."

Durell said, "Overland? By car? It's a long, long drive."

"You can do it."

"I'd rather not," Durell said.

"But you were lent to me for this purpose, Sam."

"No, thanks."

"You are afraid? Like me?"

"You're damned right I'm afraid. I wouldn't want to lose it."

"But I have prepared everything for your trip." Nuri Qam put the little casket down and wrung his hands. "I have a very powerful car, a Ferrari, and all the papers you will need. There is a secret compartment in the car in which to hide the dragon. No one can find it, and I do not think the information could be tortured from you. Me, I would babble like a brook at the first hint of pain, eh? Besides, there is Professor Berghetti, still at Qali-i-Kang."

"What about him?"

"He knows where the rest of the treasure is. It is on your way. You can get it from him. The local jail at Kang where he is being kept on charges of drug smuggling—I have friends who can arrange such things—is not beyond your ability to reach. You can pick up Berghetti and the rest of Prince Chan's treasure—nothing so consequential as the dragon, of course, but one hates to waste such important finds—and go the rest of the way to Kabul with it."

"No."

"Sam—"

"Unless you come with me."

Nuri Qam pressed his hands flat against his fat chest in an expression of horror. "I? I would only be in your way, Sam."

"You'd be my insurance policy."

"More likely, your death warrant!"

Durell waited. The exquisite room was very quiet. Dimly, from across the terrace, he heard the caged birds still chirping. Someone walked out there with a soft *slap-slap* of slippers. The moonlight touched the stone fretwork with silver and outlined the dark balconies across the terrace. The night was hot. He imagined most of the household was already tucked into their beds on the sleeping terraces, as was the custom at this time of year in Meshed.

"Sam, please help me with this. The car is out in the back, in the new garage. Keys, petrol, everything. Extra money for you in the dash compartment. There is an automatic rifle in the luggage boot. The hiding place for the box is just beyond it, against the back panel of the trunk. You press the upper right corner and at the same time you press diagonally opposite. Hide the dragon in there. Please, do this for me, Sam. Your government promised —and for old time's sake—"

The shot came from somewhere outside, on the balcony opposite across the terrace, near the bird cages.

There was no sound except for a slight, flat noise, as if a silencer had been used. The bullet was accurate enough, but Durell never knew if it was meant for him or Nuri Qam. He felt its passage next to his head and then Nuri's breath exploded in a stifled screech. Blood suddenly spattered and spread across the left shoulder of his white silk shirt. The impact of the bullet knocked the fat man sidewise and down, crashing against the inlaid cabinet from which he had taken the dragon. Durell's reaction was smooth and fast. He went spinning to the left and down, and at the same time he reached for the little casket falling from Nuri Qam's grasp.

A woman began to scream in a high, ululating voice. It was cut off abruptly, as if a knife had sliced across her throat.

Footsteps pattered across the terrace. Durell rolled over against the far well and saw Nuri Qam squirm painfully up against the cabinet, half-seated, his eyes incredulously watching the blood seep from his shoulder wound. No question about taking Nuri with him now. He slid along the tiled floor as another shot came through the fretwork, chipping stone and smashing into the wall over his head. He tried to count the pairs of footsteps racing across the terrace, but there were too many of them. The attack on the villa had come with speed, silence, efficiency, and overwhelming strength.

Durell got up, holding the box that contained the dragon, and slid through the nearest door just as the first of the attackers gained the balcony and ran for the entrance to the room. The corridor ahead was in darkness. He ran to the end, found a flight of stone steps going up and down. Cooking smells still lingered here, and he guessed the kitchen was directly below. He took two steps down, heard an angry voice in Farsi, heard a shot, a moan, then a yell of command. A massacre was taking place here.

He whirled, took the steps upward two at a time. He came to a wooden door at the top of the stone stairway, slammed against it, and fell through. The warm night air engulfed him. He was on a sleeping terrace under a striped canopy, and a huddle of white-robed figures tumbled backward from him. A woman screamed. He ignored her and moved to the rail. He could see most of the villa's walled compound from here, and the street that led back toward Meshed. Three or four cars had pulled up around the corner, and two men waited there, obviously taking care of transportation, while the others invaded the villa. Someone saw him leaning over the roof rail and raised a shout of warning. He ducked back and ran for the other side, where the women huddled. They scattered like frightened hens as he approached, perhaps more appalled by their lack of veils in his presence than by what was happening below. Shouts, screams and smashing sounds came from the lower floors.

There was a flat roof two levels below, and a driveway that looked reasonably new. Wooden gates barred the way out. Durell felt hampered by the heavy, ornate box he carried. Without it, he could have climbed down the stone fretwork, but with only one hand free, he did not care to attempt it. He turned away, heard the women scream in chorus as foosteps pounded on the stairs to the sleeping terrace, and then he slid over the rail anyway.

He had to move fast. The women would point him out to his pursuers. He wondered if they had finished off the wounded Nuri Qam, and then he concentrated on saving himself. There was an ornamental hasp on the dragon's box, and he unbuckled it and hooked it into his belt, then sought a grip on the stone carvings. He lowered himself below the rail, felt for a toehold, and went down another foot or two. The roof of the garage was still ten feet below.

He jumped.

A shout followed him from the sleeping terrace, and then he struck, his knees springy, legs loose, and rolled twice across the roof, the heavy box dangling and banging into his stomach, hitting his elbow as it swung. He came up smoothly and ran for the side of the garage roof. Another drop of about ten feet. He chose a plot of grass on this side and jumped again, arms wide for balance. Again he rolled over, came up running for the garage doors. They were not locked. The darkness inside smelled of motor oil and gasoline and the fresh scent of a new car. The Ferrari loomed like a panther in the shadows. The overhead door rolled smoothly upward without too much sound. He tossed the dragon box into the seat beside him and groped for the keys. The car was a four-seater, with luggage space behind the leather seat backs. The key was in the ignition. He heard the welcome bellow of the powerful racing engine as he turned it, threw in the clutch, shifted. The car rolled forward. Something pinged on the long, sleek hood as he came into sight of those above on the terrace. Their shouts sounded frustrated. The wooden gates loomed ahead. He did not put on the headlights. The barrier came up fast and as he hit it the lock sprung and the panels burst outward, letting him through. He was doing fifty when the front wheels hit the street—

And then something cold pressed against the back of his neck.

"Go just a bit further, Mr. Durell, and then stop."

He did not need to be told that it was a gun shoved hard against his spinal column. He heard movement from the dark shadows in the back seat behind him. He smelled sweat and perfume, curiously intermingled. Two of them.

"Zhirnov?" he asked.

"Be careful of your driving. Turn right here. Yes, that's

it. Go toward the sports stadium. It's empty tonight. Yes, now slow down. We don't want to give the police an excuse for a speeding ticket, now, do we?"

"Anya, is that you?" he asked.

"Yes," she whispered.

"You arranged with Zhirnov to do this?"

"Not exactly, but—"

Zhirnov's voice was like a slither of cold steel. "Be quiet. Stop the car now, Durell."

There were empty fields on one side of the road, a row of new concrete apartment buildings in various stages of construction to the left.

"Pull in there," Zhirnov said. The pressure of his gun on the back of Durell's neck was relentless. "Yes, just there, the other side of the bulldozer."

Durell did as he was told. He braked the Ferrari, looked into the rear-vision mirror, saw that the road was empty. No help in sight. Nothing he could do. He swore softly and wheeled the purring car onto the jolting, rutted ground of the construction site.

"Anya—" he began.

"Shut up," Zhirnov said. "The box, please. The dragon. Nuri Qam had it all the time, eh?"

"Yes."

"A fat, disgusting thief. Nothing more than a thief."

"And you?" Durell asked. "What are you?"

"No better than yourself, *Gospodin* Durell. Anya, take the box. You did well. It will help to cancel out the other mistakes you have made. Take it, Anya."

Durell stopped the car in the shadows of the parked bulldozer. If there were any watchmen on the construction site, they must all be asleep, he thought. He reached for the box beside him and handed it backward, careful not to turn his head against the cold warning of Zhirnov's weapon.

"Anya, I trusted you," he said.

"No, you did not. Not at any time."

Her fingers exerted a curious pressure against his as she took the box from his hand. Suddenly he knew that Zhirnov was going to pull the trigger and blow him out of existence. He could smell the man's intense hostility, smell the immediate danger inside the car. Every nerve in him screamed a protest against instant oblivion. He moved his elbow against the door latch and pressed downward with it as he talked.

"Zhirnov, I hear that Colonel Skoll, Anya's boss, is in prison somewhere in Moscow. Who do you really work for? Is it General Goroschev? The whole world knows he's a hawk, anxious to precipitate a showdown with your Chinese neighbors. You want the dragon just to infuriate Peking and bring about that sort of confrontation, don't you?"

"It is necessary," Zhirnov said flatly. "Sooner or later, it will come. Now is a better time than later. So be quiet. Anya, open the box."

"I can't," she said.

"It has no key?"

"No key. There must be a secret way to open it."

Zhirnov said tightly, "Do you know how to open the box, Durell?"

"Yes."

"Do so, then. It would be a pity to destroy such a fine work of art."

"Give it to me," Durell said.

He heard movement in the narrow back seat behind him. At the same moment, for just a moment, the pressure of the gun was eased against the nape of his neck. It was now or never. He moved, pushing his weight against the unlatched car door, and at the same time he fell to the left, out toward the ground. There came an oath, a deafening crash in his ear as Zhirnov's gun went off. All in an instant, Durell rolled away, heaving himself to one side. He used the car as his shield, aiming for the shelter of the parked bulldozer next to the Ferrari. But Zhirnov was like a huge cat. He came out of the car in a blur of speed, jumping for Durell. His feet hit Durell in the small of the back, sent him forward, his hands scraping on the rough gravel. He tried to turn and rise to face Zhirnov, reaching upward at the same time for the gun in the other man's hand. He knew in that moment that he had tried and failed. From the corner of his eye he saw Anya come out of the car and move behind Zhirnov. He could not see the expression on the Russian's face. He heard Zhirnov grunt, saw the man's gun rise, and tried to duck. He felt a smashing pain on the side of his neck, struck back, felt a cartilage break in the man's nose, and then, with Anya's face swimming in the background, he went down and out.

14

He awoke and thought he was drowning.

He coughed, and massive pain soared through his head. He tried to sit up against the deluge of water in his face, and strong, quiet hands pushed him back. He finally realized that someone was trying to give him a drink of water and that it was spilling down over his nose and mouth and chin. He opened his mouth and swallowed gratefully. His head pounded harder. His head, shoulder and hips felt as if he were lying on rocks. When he opened his eyes, he saw the night sky and dim stars that reeled and danced away. He closed his eyes and someone said, "Oh, Sam."

"What?"

"Can you hear me, Sam?"

There was a sound like repetitive thunder in his ears. It was his own pulse. He opened his eyes again and struggled up upon his elbows. The effort seemed enormous.

"I hear you," he said.

"I am happy. Oh, I am happy. I thought you were dead."

"*Anya?*"

"Hush. Call me Annie."

"Why?"

"The others might hear."

"What others?"

129

"Howard and George and Lucy."

"What are you talking about, Anya?"

"Annie," she said. "They think I'm American."

"But you're not," he said.

"*They* are."

"How do you know that?"

"You'll see. Can you sit up all the way now? And don't forget, call me Annie."

"All right. Annie."

He sat up. It took quite an effort. The throbbing in the back of his head increased, as if a sledge hammer was trying to pound him down upon the rocky bed on which he lay. He took a few deep breaths, and Anya knelt beside him, her face anxious, solicitous, in the gloom. He did not know where he was. He smelled liquor, and realized that someone had poured a bottle of cheap Iranian wine all over him.

Anya said, "I tried to make it look as if you were drunk."

"Why?"

"For the others. I told you. Howard and George and Lucy. Americans. After I hit Pigam—"

"You hit Zhirnov?"

"Yes, I did." She bit her lip. "It was to save you. He was going to kill you, of course."

"Of course," Durell said.

"And then I got you away from the bulldozer and a car came along, a van, and I signalled to it and they stopped when they saw me. It was Howard and George and Lucy, people I had met when we were working at Berghetti's dig in Afghanistan. I told them at first that you were sick from drinking too much. The bottle of wine was in the Ferrari, along with sandwiches that Nuri Qam must have prepared for you. I had time to pour most of the wine over you. They believed me."

"And Zhirnov?"

"He got away."

"And the dragon?"

"He took it with him."

"You're lying, Anya."

"Annie. No, I'm not lying. Please do not call me Anya. They used to know me as Annie. I was out on the road with you, talking to the people in the van, and they were going to Afghanistan again and they offered to give me a lift and to help you, too. When I went back to the area where the car was, Zhirnov was totally gone. And the box with the dragon. Was the dragon really in the box?"

"Yes," he said. "You're lying."

"No, Sam."

"Why did you save my life?"

She stood up. "If you talk like that, I may regret what I did to help you."

"Where did Zhirnov go?"

"I don't know. Into the unfinished apartment building, I think." She shrugged. "I was not inclined to chase after him, dragon or no dragon."

He got to his feet. The smell of wine on his clothing made him nauseated. Or maybe it was his headache. He staggered and finally caught some measure of equilibrium. He was in a pebbly ditch about eight feet below the level of the road. It seemed a difficult climb to the top. He breathed deeply again and slowly began to feel better. There seemed to be nothing in sight in the darkness around them. The van was a Chevy, painted a bright yellow, battered and dusty around the edges. Standing about at the front of the van were three young people, smoking and drinking from a common wine bottle. They seemed at ease. The road here was paved, but he saw that a hundred yards farther on it turned to dirt, although it was reasonably well graded.

"Where are we?"

"We've gone through the checkpoint at the Iranian frontier at Youssafabad. I showed them your papers; I told them you were drunk. I had your visa and vaccination folders, and Howie has the green auto insurance and triptique papers. There was no trouble at all. Howard seems very competent. Right now we're on a sort of a no-man's land, not far from Islam Qala, on the Afghan frontier. About a mile ahead. Are you all right, Sam?"

"No," he said.

"What is it?"

"I'd like to know where Zhirnov is," he said. "And the dragon."

The three young people greeted him casually, with no undue curiosity. They had accepted Anya as an old comrade from the Berghetti dig, where they had worked several weeks together. Howard, the driver and owner of the van, was the tallest and the oldest, with longish hair and knowing, sober eyes. George was shorter, partly bald, and what was left of his hair trailed down his back in a pigtail. He was missing a front tooth. The girl, Lucy, was rather homely, but with a rich and mature figure, and it was plain that she was having the time of her life, enjoying the services of two young men. They all wore blue jeans.

"Hi," they said in chorus.

"Hello," Durell said.

"Welcome aboard," Howard said. "Shall we go on?"

They all seemed well-educated, chattering in the syndromes of their college courses. Each had decided to take a year from their classrooms to travel in Asia. They accepted Durell cheerfully, without restraint, but it was plain that because he was more mature than they, he was considered an outsider. The interior of the van was reasonably tidy—Lucy would one day make some man a good housewife, he reckoned, after this fling. The vehicle was equipped with a small gas stove, bedrolls, and built-in clothing chests.

"Make yourself comfortable," Howard said. They did not offer their last names. "And lay off the booze, huh? It's bad stuff out here."

"Thank you."

"No need. Any friend of Annie's, you know."

"Where are you headed for?"

"Back to the Seistan. There might be more work at the digs. We heard Berghetti is out of the slammer and looking for some more relics. The pay is good, anyway. Are you going anywhere in particular?"

"The Seistan is good enough for me," Durell said.

"You don't look like a digger," Lucy said.

"I'm not."

"A wandering flower child? You're a few years too late." Lucy giggled.

"I guess so."

"Sad," said George.

They had no trouble at the frontier checkpoint of Islam Qala, although they had to turn out of the van and stand by while armed customs men turned the van inside out in a search for contraband and drugs. The van was clean. The guards seemed disappointed. They tried to object to the two guns they found—a Remington .30-30 hunting rifle belonging to bald George, and Durell's .38. They wanted a bribe, since the carrying of weapons for "sport" was on the approved list. Durell spoke to them in Dari and gave them several thousand Afghani notes from his dwindling hoard, and the objections changed to smiles and they were waved on, with warnings against road robbers.

"You were too generous," Lucy said. "That was enough to keep us in chow all week. How come you have so much bread?"

"It's what is left of my severance pay when I quit my job," Durell said.

"Yes? What kind of job?"

"I'm finished with it," Durell said. "It was slowly killing me."

It was past midnight, and except for an occasional truck, there was no other traffic on the highway. It was over a hundred kilometers to Herat, where they had to turn south on the only passable road round the wildly mountainous Hazarat. Northward in the night were the dim outlines of the Firoz-Koh foothills—mountains that stretched in a long, cruel barrier across the waist of the country until they lifted into the incredible peaks of the Hindu Kush, far to the east.

Plainly, the subculture in which these youths moved was an extremely private one. They were friendly enough, but Durell could not find a chink in their armor. They were definitely American, not camouflaged Soviet agents. When he was finally satisfied about it, from listening to their murmuring conversation, he let Anya persuade him to rest on one of the sleeping bags, and he fell almost instantly asleep.

Just before he slipped off, he felt Anya's hand slide into his and grip his fingers.

She was shaking his shoulder urgently.

"Sam, wake up. Are you awake?"

"Yes, I'm awake."

The Chevy van was stopped. Howard and George and Lucy were sitting on the front bench seat, talking in low voices. There was a hubbub of sound up ahead.

"Sam, the Ferrari just went past us."

"Zhirnov?"

"Going like a bat out of hell, as you would say."

"You're sure it was Zhirnov?"

"Yes, I had a look at him. He seems to be alone."

"Why have we stopped?"

"There's been a bus accident. It hit a camel. We're just beyond Zindajan, about twenty miles from Herat."

He sat up. Lucy turned her homely face on her long neck and pushed back her long hair. Her smile was gentle. "You must have been tired, Mr. Durell."

"Sam," he said. "Call me Sam."

"All right, Mr. Durell. Sam. Want some coffee?"

He got out of the back of the van and stood on the paved all-weather road outside of Herat. The eastern sky was pale with a new dawn. Northward, the Paropamisus mountains loomed against the dimming stars. To the right was a long valley, where the Hari River flowed between watered fields and clumps of feathery trees. The river looked like steel in the pale light. There was grunting and shouting up ahead as some men tried to remove a dead camel from the highway. The bus that had struck the animal was a Qaderi Lines vehicle. A truck had stopped behind the van now, and its engine growled irregularly as the driver revved the throttle with an impatient foot. The air felt crisp, a refreshing change from the humid heat they had left earlier. His head still ached, but the intensity of the throbbing had lessened. He felt better.

The camel was as obstinate dead as it had been when alive. Its weight resisted the efforts of the people from the bus to remove it from the road. He walked back and spoke to Howard, who sat behind the driver's wheel.

"Why don't we just go around the bus?"

"Man, we're not in a hurry."

"Howie, I'm anxious to get on with it. Did you see a Ferrari go by us, while I slept?"

"Five minutes ago. A beauty. Doing ninety."

"I'd like to catch up with that man. It's a personal thing. Can't we get going?"

"You've got to forget your stateside tempo out here, Mr. Durell. Relax with it, man. You're not running around Madison Avenue now. Anyway, we figure on spending a couple of days in Herat. Lucy's a history major, and the city's supposed to have interesting architecture, the Friday mosque, lots of culture. We'll be there soon."

Durell decided not to argue. The camel was finally off the road. The argument was still going on between the bus driver and the owner of the strayed beast. Durell went to the back of the van and spoke to Anya.

"You're quite sure it was Zhirnov?"

"Yes."

"Did he spot you?"

"I think not."

"Why would he come back here into Afghanistan?"

"I don't know. Maybe to find Professor Berghetti."

"Why Berghetti?"

"I don't know," Anya said.

Ten minutes later they were moving again. They went through a toll gate and a small village with the distinctive windmills that marked the Herat region. The fields looked rich and productive. The air remained sharp and clear as the sun came up in their eyes. Howard made one more stop, at a local *chaikana* where they picked up tea and used the facilities. By nine o'clock they were in Herat, after crossing the Pul-i-Malan, the 10th century bridge

over the Hari River. Lucy was the guide for the group.
She put on a pair of huge round sunglasses that somehow
added to her gooselike look and told them about Gazar-
gah, the little religious village built around the ruins of the
Queen's Tomb with its six surviving minarets, and about
the mystic poet Khaja Ansari. Durell forced himself to be
patient. His business was often a hurry-up-and-wait
proposition.

Howard found a small hotel in the Old City on the
Shari-i-Nau, north of the city wall. Herat had a placid
air, even in the Covered Bazaar and the tree-lined boulevard going toward the plush Governor's Palace in the
New Town. Their rooms were simple, neat and clean.
Taxis and pedestrians made a quiet hum of sound in the
narrow streets. Lucy bought cheese and yoghurt and nuts,
fresh bread with a crisp crust, and dried fruit. They ate in
her room. The tall, thin girl added a few drops of Clorox
from a large bottle to make the water potable.

"Did you know," Lucy said, "that this place was settled
over 2500 years ago by a Persian people called the Hai-
vara? They were running from the Assyrians. Fantastic.
Alexander rebuilt the ruins, but everybody wanted a piece
of the Khorassan—it's rich and fertile, you see. Scythians,
Khushans, Hephtalite Huns—you name them. Then the
Arabs came in 663, the Saminids, the Ghazni dynasties,
the kings of Ghor and Khwarezm. Sounds like fairy tales,
right? And of course, Genghis Khan in 1221, he killed
12,000 people here. We really have to give this place a
good look, at the stuff left by the Timurids after Tamer-
lane came along. The Citadel, of course. The Covered
Wells, the craft shops near the Friday mosque. We could
learn something about their handicrafts, maybe use it
when we go home." Lucy was obviously the energizer of
the trio. She poked her round glasses up on her long nose.
"Did you see some of the women here in the *chaudris?*
Like big black bats, hurrying along. It's all fantastic. We'll
have to spend a couple of days here."

"I'll pass," Durell said.

They looked at him over their breakfast. Lucy said,

"Still with the Madison Avenue syndrome, Mr. Durell? Time—"

"Time means everything. I'll see you later."

Anya said, "I'll go with you, Sam."

"Of course." At the hotel room door, Durell turned and asked, "How do you people know that Professor Berghetti is out of the slammer and back to work at his Seistan dig again?"

Lucy's smile reflected tolerance of an older generation. "Oh," she said, "word just gets around."

15

He had no luck.

At the Ariana Airlines office he learned that no planes flew to Chakhansur in the Seistan for two days. The office windows faced a tree-shaded plaza with pistachio trees growing on tidy lawns. The Ariana clerk seemed surprised that anyone would want to fly to Chakhansur. He offered a flight to Kandahar in the southeast, but a map assured Durell that the distance to the lakes was too great. He tried the Bakhtar Afghan Airlines with even worse results. The place was closed. Anya clung to his hand as he searched out the bus offices. A bus went from Herat to Chakhansur via Farah, but arrival was not promised in less than three days. Durell thought of Zhirnov racing south in the Ferrari, and gave it up. He was about to turn away, when the bus clerk said,

"Sir? My brother."

"Who?"

"My brother Mazar. Mazar Khumri. A taxi service. Ordinarily, he works out of the Tourist Office across from the Tomb of Abulqazam, but he can be found at this hour of the morning next to the jeweler who makes lapiz-lazuli items—very beautiful—in the bazaar. Mazar Khumri, that is his name. He will be very reasonable. An excellent guide, too. We were both born in Khash. It is very bad country down there, sir. The desert and the Dasht-i-Margo are full of thieves and murderers. And the mountain roads require a practiced driver. I recommend Mazar. He will take good care of you, sir."

They took a *ghazni,* one of the decorated horse carriages along the Shar-i-Nau, around the looming mass of the 15th-century Citadel, glowering against the clean blue sky, and around the Friday Mosque, with its blaze of tiled walls and minarets, designed in flowers and vines and complex geometric designs. Passing through the narrow walled streets with willow trees and children playing in the shade, they came to the Char-Suq, with its open workrooms of weavers and cabinetmakers. On the next street to the east were the jewelers.

Once again, luck was against them.

"Mazar?" the man said. "He has gone to Kabul. Just this morning, with a party of Swedish tourists."

"You are quite sure?"

"My uncle Muzzaffa might help you. You can find him at the petrol station just behind Jami's Tomb, on the Meshed Road. It is not hard to find. Tell him Ibrahim sent you, sir. Very reliable. Better than Mazar, I assure you."

Durell gave up.

He had two phone calls to make, after a stop at the Pashtany Bank to change his Iranian currency. He counted his receipts with care. Later, he found a public phone at the Herat Hotel, a modern place with a new swimming pool. His luck changed. The operator managed to get a connection to Meshed across the border within fifteen minutes. Anya waited near the booth, watching the tourists in the lobby. She looked pale and uncertain, as if she did not know her future or even her immediate destination. She had committed herself against Zhirnov, and it meant self-exile and perhaps assassination in the days to come, wherever she fled. Just now, she clung to him for safety while deciding where her loyalties lay. He did not envy her.

Finally the telephone was picked up in Nuri Qam's villa in Meshed.

"*Sob bekheyr*," a man said in Farsi. "Good morning."

"I'd like to speak to Mr. Qam, please."

"I am sorry, Mr. Qam is in Tehran."

"I mean Mr. Nuri Qam."

"Not here, sir. Who is calling?"

"Is he in the hospital?"

There was a pause. The voice changed. "I am Mr. Qam's personal secretary. Why should he be in a hospital, sir? Who are you?"

"My call is urgent," Durell said. He gave his name. "If Mr. Qam is available, I must speak with him."

There was a much longer pause this time. Then, "*Kheyli khoub*. Very well. Please wait."

Again it seemed like a long time. Durell watched Anya in the hotel lobby. She stood with her arms crossed against her breast, in a defensive posture. Her eyes looked frightened, although the lobby seemed normal. She turned and looked at Durell in the booth and he smiled and lifted a hand to reassure her. She moved closer to him. He didn't mind if she overheard his conversation.

Finally the telephone clicked.

"Nuri?"

"Ah, Sam, Sam. I am in great pain."

"But alive," Durell said.

"Allah was kind. Where are you?"

"Herat."

"You have the—the item? You should be beyond Herat by now."

Durell said, "I don't have the dragon any more." He told Nuri Qam what had happened in succinct detail, not pausing while the man groaned and interjected angry exclamations. "No use crying about it now, Nuri."

"You say he has the dragon *and* the Ferrari?"

"Yes."

"Perhaps you can catch up to him on the way south."

"I intend to try. Why should he go south, Nuri?"

"How would I know his mind, Sam? I gave the dragon

into your custody, and you promptly lost it. I warn you of repercussions to your government if you do not recover it promptly. After all these days of anxiety, I trusted you completely. You have failed me, Sam. I am disappointed. Your arrival here was a disaster. The attack on the villa was completely organized. I have lost three servants, killed in the raid, and my brother's daughter. They were ruthless, with no compassion. I myself am most fortunate to be still alive, thanks to Allah. The wound is painful, but not serious."

"Nuri, I accept responsibility for the dragon."

"You think you can recover it? You have a lead? Ah, you are clever. Yes, yes. You revive my hopes. I have been desolate. Such a thing of beauty. It belongs to my nation, Sam. You will get it and take it on to Kabul? I can give you instructions about the archives and the museum—"

"Later," Durell said. "I'll be in touch. Now, what about Berghetti?"

Nuri's voice changed slightly. "What about him?"

"He still seems to be in the picture. There seems to be evidence that he's not in jail, as you said."

"Nonsense. He must be. When you recover the dragon, you must call me, then go to Qali-i-Kang and I will arrange for Berghetti to be released into your custody. Further instructions will follow."

"All right. Take care, Nuri."

"I will, I will."

Durell got a second call through to Sarah Fingal's apartment in Meshed. For four rings, the phone was not picked up, and he was afraid she could not be reached. Then he heard her quiet, subdued voice.

"Oh, Sam, are you all right?"

"Not really, Sarah. I need more help."

"I really don't want any more to do with this. I've been in touch with General Wellington. The man is a beast. This affair killed Homer, and he doesn't seem to care a bit." She paused. "What do you want from me now?"

"Check back with McFee in Washington. I want all the latest in Nuri Qam's dossier. If K Section doesn't have it, NSA's computer at Fort Meade will, I'm sure."

"Just what are you looking for?"

"Nuri Qam's brother has allegedly been in Tehran. Name is E. Dochi Chagha Qam. He's an art collector. You might also get the latest rundown on Nuri's background, his travels in recent years, political associates, his problems in Kabul."

"Is something wrong about Nuri?"

"Something is wrong with everybody in this thing, Sarah. Will you do this for me?"

"I will," she said reluctantly. "For Homer's sake. How will I get in touch with you?"

"I'll call you from Qali-i-Kang."

"That's a godforsaken place."

"That's where the dragon was found," Durell said.

His luck continued to improve. He took Anya back to the hotel and found the young trio, Howard and George and Lucy, desolate. They were the usual run of American student wanderers; their lines of survival still ran back to the bank accounts of their establishment parents.

Lucy had lost their money.

The little hotel room was thick with their gloom. Lucy was weeping, doing a *mea culpa* bit, and the tears had not improved her few attractions. Her long nose was red, her hair disheveled. She sat cross-legged on the floor by the window, while George, with his pigtail awry, berated her. She looked as if the world had dissolved under her feet.

"I don't know *what* happened!" she protested, and hiccupped. "One minute I had the purse, the next it was *gone!* I don't even know when it disappeared or was taken."

George pulled at his pigtail nervously. "You bitch, I can't ask for more money from back home, right now."

"I know," Lucy said ruefully.

Durell spoke from the doorway. "So you'll have to skip sightseeing here in Herat, okay?"

Lucy looked tearful. "What do you mean?"

"I'll pay you—the three of you—a thousand dollars to take Annie and me south—as fast as you can drive."

"Jesus, a capitalist," George sneered.

Durell said, "The local fuzz doesn't take kindly to young Americans who are broke and ready to panhandle. This place is the Ritz compared to the local jail. They'll probably slap a drug smuggling charge on you, too, unless you come up with a heavy bribe of bread, which you can't do."

Lucy hiccupped again. "I wanted to see Herat—"

"Another time," Durell said. "We'll get gas and an extra jerry can and be on our way. Right now,"

Lucy climbed awkwardly to her feet. Her shoulders were slumped. George looked greedy. Howard was amused.

"All right, Mr. Durell," Lucy said mournfully.

16

It was two hundred miles from Herat to Chakhansur near the border, beyond Farah; the latter half of the way was on a dubious secondary road. The distance was deceptive. There were river fords along the Harut River, mountain passes toward Sadzawar, where the eastern peaks lifted to 12,000 feet. More mountain passes at Farah, and then the Khash Desert, through which the Khash River flowed to lose itself in the salt marshes and the Helmand lakes. The Afghanis were building dams along the Helmand and Khash-Rud, to the annoyance of the Iranians in the Seistan *ostan* across the border. The best bus schedule, as Durell had discovered, was a journey of about three days by road. And at the end of it was the Dasht-i-Margo, another desert of burning bare rock and sand, before they could reach Qali-i-Kang near the junction of the Helmand and Khash Rivers.

They left Herat at noon, heading south. The girls slept in the back of the van while Durell took the wheel from Howard. The two young men sat in sullen silence beside him. Altogether, Durell estimated they were at least ten hours behind Zhirnov in the Ferrari. But the Ferrari was not built for the questionable roads ahead, and its highway speed would be negated as they moved south.

The van had surprising power, and he negotiated the

rising hills and twisting passes south of Chahar Burjak with no problems. The mild weather of Herat soon yielded to a harsh heat raised by the flashing, reflected sunlight on bare, scorched rock. The temperature began to drop as they climbed up through the first mountain passes. Durell took the hairpin turns fast, to the point where both Howard and George looked a bit fearful. The road itself was not the only hazard. There were no railroads in Afghanistan, and commercial traffic was by truck, and the truck drivers drove with hair-raising abandon that created problems whenever one came their way. Durell's face was set. He did not slacken speed at any time, whatever games of chicken the oppositing drivers tried to play.

It was during a relatively quiet interlude that George pulled out the antenna of a powerful shortwave radio receiver, sat it on his lap, and thrust the antenna out of the van window and began to fiddle with the dials—presumably to get his mind off Durell's driving. Their elevation at the time was quite high, south of Chahur Burjak, and reception was loud and clear. For a few moments, they picked up Turkomen and Russian stations, then for just an instant as George idly turned the dials, Durell heard the flat no-nonsense news reports in Mandarin from Peking.

"Turn it back," he said.

"It's just Chinese. You understand Chinese?"

"He does," Howard said. "Like me. Maybe he learned it in Nam."

"Man, what are you, Durell?" George complained. "Some kind of cop, or something?"

"No."

"A spook, then. Anybody who understands Chinese—"

"Turn it back, Georgie," Howard said.

The news report came in crisply. It recounted the accidental death of General Chan Wei-Wu in a Peking suburb from a gunshot wound. The Deputy Chairman expressed his regrets. A Madame Strelsky was also a victim of the shooting. A successor to the General would shortly be named to the General's post. And that was all.

Durell nodded to George, who promptly picked up a

pseudo-rock band from Bucharest. Durell wondered what was really happening in Peking. But it occurred to him that nothing would stop Mr. Chou from continuing his search for the dragon unless he, too, learned the news.

It was past noon when they came down into the valley of the Harut for their first ford of the shallow, rippling river. Five miles later, as they climbed the opposite hills toward Qali Adraskan, they came upon the Ferrari.

The wreck was about a mile away. Apparently Zhirnov, no Grand Prix driver, had taken a wrong turn onto a road that petered out into a goat track along a barren spine of the mountains. Durell turned off also, to follow the track, driving with care. Except for the one spot from which he had spotted the wreck, it was invisible from the main highway. Up here, the wind was still like a blast furnace, and the sun's heat bounced off the glittering rocks in waves of fury. No one was in sight. Far below, he glimpsed the winding curves of the Harut Rud. There was a small village at a bend where a local dam had been built. But where the Ferrari lay was only a place for goats and wandering tribesmen.

Possibly hyenas, too, Durell thought as he braked the van. The wreck could not have occurred more than a few hours ago, yet the Ferrari had been picked clean of every removable part by human scavengers.

He picked up Howard's Remington and stepped down to the hot stony path, fifty yards from where the sports car rested without wheels, tires, and possibly even the engine.

"I thought you were in a hurry," Howard asked.

"I am. But there's a time for care, too."

"Nobody's around," George said petulantly.

"We don't know that."

"I heard these hills are dangerous," Lucy observed.

"Yes. Stay in the van. You, too, Annie."

Anya shook her head. "No, I'll go with you."

A high cliff of soft stone loomed to the south, the rock reddish, reflecting the white sky with a bloody glare. The cliff was eroded by several canyons, filled with crumbled rock, that led upward to the farther summit.

"Zhirnov wouldn't still be here," Anya murmured.

He gave her the rifle. "Just the same, cover me. If not Zhirnov, there may be a few tribesmen who don't care for strangers poaching on their territory."

"But we're wasting time—"

"There's a Kalashnikov automatic in the Ferrari that I don't think anyone could have found," he said. "And I want it."

But the deck over the Ferrari's luggage space had been removed, he saw. He walked closer, careful of his footing on the treacherous shale. Nothing green grew here. Certainly there was no reason for Zhirnov to have turned off, except through error. The wind made a thin whining sound as it came down the narrow canyons nearby.

"But where did he go?" Anya murmured. "If he wasn't hurt in the wreck, maybe local tribesmen took him—"

"No signs of violence," Durell said. "Zhirnov would land on his feet somehow, go south in some way."

He came to a halt beside the wrecked car. Something was wrong in the atmosphere, but he could not define it. He listened to the wind and felt the hot sun on the nape of his neck. He walked around the car, not touching anything. There was no blood on the leather seats, no bullet holes, though the glass on the right side doors were starred and shattered. The stony ground yielded no footprints. He came back to the rear of the wreck and looked deep into the open trunk, remembering the secret compartments Nuri Qam had described, the method of pressing at opposite diagonal corners to get at the automatic rifle and the storage compartment there. Both flaps were open. He felt inside. No gun. No dragon box. His fingers ran rapidly around the edges of the secret flaps. No gouges, knife marks, nothing to indicate that the small doors in the luggage area had been forced open.

He straightened—and the sound of a single rifle came with a sharp, rolling report that echoed back and forth from the rocky mountainside.

The bullet hit the car with a sharp thud. Durell dived for Anya and threw her flat to the stony ground. The girl gasped, moved under his weight, tried to rise.

"Keep down," he snapped.

"Is it—Zhirnov?"

"Maybe just thieves, hill people."

They waited. In the van behind them, the trio of young people watched with puzzlement. They did not get out of the vehicle. He carefully raised his head and surveyed the washed-out canyons. He saw nothing. Sunlight flashed on the sharp bits of rock that littered the slopes. Any of the glintings could have been the reflection off a rifle barrel. He raised himself up.

"Crawl under the car, Anya. It will be safer."

She said, "You feel you must protect me?"

"Why not?"

"Then you must trust me now?"

He was not about to engage in that topic just at the moment. When the girl rolled under the protection of the car, he stood up and raced for the nearest canyon mouth, using a zigzag direction to confuse the ambushers. But there were no other shots. Except for the wind and the swift crunch of his boots on the shale, there was no sound. He paused, clearly exposed, aware of something very wrong.

"Zhirnov!" he called.

The reply was little more than a groan.

"It is I. Chou. That was my last bullet."

Durell swore and scrambled up the rocky slope toward the voice. His gun was ready, and he was aware of the danger of a trap, of imminent death. He climbed on.

He found Mr. Chou, the Chinese Black House agent, behind a large boulder that was precariously balanced against the tilted rubble filling the canyon. The stout Chinese lay on his back, and the rifle he had used for his single ambush shot had fallen away, out of reach. The man's white suit was dusty and torn, and one of the round lenses in his glasses was broken. Durell bent and removed the rifle and checked the action. The chamber was empty. He tossed the weapon away and knelt beside Chou.

"What happened here?"

"Death has come to me here," Chou said. He made a face of pain. "Not unexpected. But it is very painful. I was shot in the back."

"Zhirnov?"

"He escaped. I do not—know where."

"You tried to ambush him?"

"I—Freyda and I—yes. We knew he was coming this way. I had some greedy tribesmen with me. They preferred to loot the car to doing what I paid them to do." Mr. Chou moved his round head in negation. "My legs are not mine. The sun grows dim. I wish I had reached you with my last shot. I waited and waited. I directed the tribesmen to set up false barricades on the highway and led him here. But Zhirnov was too quick."

"Where did he go?"

"I do not know. I—"

Durell said flatly, "But it was all useless, Chou. The General is dead. The report came over the Peking radio. He and his mistress are dead. Did you know she was Freyda's sister? The hawks in Peking have no leader now. You have no employer. There will be no further pressures from Peking over the dragon."

Chou was silent a long time. Durell thought he was dead. Then his eyes blinked. "This is the truth?"

"I would not lie to you now."

"But the dragon—"

"Zhirnov has it."

The man's breathing was erratic, and Durell could see the pool of blood under his back, where the shot that had finished him broke his spine.

Durell said, "You're sure Freyda was taken?"

"Yes." Chou had trouble breathing. "My grandfather—I was a little boy—belonged to old China. He was full of moral maxims. 'A single false move loses the game,' he would say. Or, 'Knowledge is boundless; but one man's capacity is limited.' I thought I had forgotten those sayings . . . The General is truly dead?"

"Yes. According to Peking radio."

" 'The mischief of fire or water or robbers touch only

the body,' my grandfather used to say. 'But those of evil doctrines destroy the mind.' The old man often told me stories about lucky tortoises and dragons. I would have liked to see this particular dragon. 'A man without thought for tomorrow will have sorrow today.' "

Mr. Chou stared blindly up into the glaring sun. His smile was a child's smile, of faraway remembrance. "The old man told me how P'an Ku, a sculptor who lived for eighteen thousand years, fashioned the world with his hammer and chisel. While he built the mountains and scooped out the seas and hollowed the river courses, P'an Ku's eternal companions were the four auspicious beasts, the Dragon, the Unicorn, the Tortoise and the Phoenix. The dragon heads all the creatures; he is larger than large, smaller than small. His breath is a cloud on which he rides up to Heaven. The Dragon has five colors in his body, and owns a pearl which is the soul of the moon. He can be visible or invisible. In the spring, he rides the clouds; in the summer he swims in deep waters . . ." Mr. Chou's voice trailed off. He smiled again. "I would have liked to see this dragon we all pursued. I would like to see my old grandfather again—"

The Chinese made a thin sound in his throat. He smiled at Durell, a sad, sad smile, filled with doubts and regrets. His eyes turned up and remained fixed on the harsh sky. A vulture soared up there.

The man was dead.

Durell turned and looked down the narrow valley. Anya was climbing up from below. He decided to wait until she joined him, and he watched her small figure move among the rocks that had spilled at the base of the canyon. Nothing else stirred except for dust devils kicked up by the whimpering wind. The air felt suddenly cooler. He thought of Chou, and how each man turned back to his origins at the moment of his end. Anya appeared and disappeared among the huge boulders. He felt a sadness for Mr. Chou and for a world of men that never found peace until the end came. Would peace for all men come with the desolate peace of a dead, radioactive world? He shrugged off a shudder and knelt beside the dead Chinese to search the man's pockets.

He heard a small scream, quickly stifled, from Anya.

She had come only halfway up among the rocks on the slope to meet him, the last time he saw her. Now he could not spot her down there.

"Anya?" he called.

His voice echoed in the narrow canyon. Down below, he saw Howard and George talking, standing beside the parked van. Anya did not reappear.

"Anya?" he called again.

He thought he glimpsed movement among the boulders where she had last been climbing, but he wasn't sure, and he left Chou's body and started down toward her, sensing the hostility of these bleak Afghan hills. Stony rubble rattled away from under his boots. He moved wide to the right, not retracing the way he had come up. Great reddish rocks towered above his head. It was like being lost in a stone forest. He could not see more than a few yards in any direction, and he turned downhill toward the center of the rock spill.

"Sam!"

Her muffled shout, quite near him, was quickly cut off. At the same moment, he heard the whisper of secret sound above and behind him. Anya's warning came too late. He felt the shock of heavy weight as a man crashed down on his shoulders; he staggered, slipped in the rubbled shale, went down on one knee, his right hand and gun flung out to keep his balance. A booted foot crushed his wrist on the stone. He smelled sweat and rancid sheepskin. Something smashed against his head and drove him over on his side. His opponent was a giant, bearded and wild-looking, his teeth showing in a cruel grin. Durell tried to draw up a knee, failed, felt something hit the nape of his neck. The mountains reeled. The earth heaved under him. He had lost his gun. He suddenly thought that this was the way it was going to end, after all, here in these empty mountains, victim of a simple, sly ambush set by tribesmen.

He heard more booted feet rush toward him and then he was buried under the weight of several evil-smelling men, and a torrent of blows rained down on him. He thought he heard Anya scream again, and a quick burst of sound from the van's engine, far below. They were running away, he thought dimly.

Then there came a last blow, and he slid inevitably into a darkness that was almost welcome.

17

It was dark and cold.

His teeth were chattering, and with a great effort he clenched his jaw against the spasms of pain in his face. The pain grew as he crawled slowly up out of unconsciousness. He did not move. Perhaps someone would notice that his teeth were not noisy any more, but the cold shook him like an aspen in the wind. One side of him was warm, pressed against something smooth and yielding. It was a woman's urgent body. He felt an arm around him, holding him close to the rounded heat. A naked leg and thigh closed over him, as if to impart the warmth of blood and living tissue to his own.

He tried to give no hint of being awake again. He lay on his left side, with the woman spooned behind him, and when he opened his eyes, he thought he had been blinded, because he saw nothing at all, only a blackness unrelieved by even the faintest glimmer of light. Gradually he became aware of the smell of poorly tanned goatskins, of stale goat's milk, of camel-dung smoke from cooking fires. The wind made flapping sounds, as if something were loosely blowing; there was a wooden creaking, too. He realized that he and the woman were lying inside a pitch-dark tent, in a place exposed to bitter mountain winds. His every muscle ached; there was a special pain in his ribs, and if several were not broken, they were at least badly bruised. His left hand throbbed where his attacker's boot had stamped on it. He carefully tried to move his fingers. They worked all right, if stiffly and painfully.

The woman wriggled against him, as if to get even closer to impart her warmth to his battered body.

"Anya?" he whispered.

He did not move when he spoke. He had pitched it too low, and he spoke her name again. "Anya?"

Her body came away from him with a startled, sudden thrust and jerk. He felt the chill wind against his back where she had been pressing against him.

"Sam?"

"Hush. Keep your voice down."

"I thought—I thought you were dying."

"Not yet," he said grimly. "And you?"

"I'm c-cold."

"They took your clothes away?"

"Every stitch. I'm sorry. I didn't mean to—"

"Please. Just whisper. Is there a guard?"

"Outside the tent."

"Come back. We might as well warm each other."

"I—now I am embarrassed."

He turned over, very carefully, testing his limbs and muscles. Nothing seemed to be broken or torn. On his right side now, he could see a glimmer of reddish light, in a long slit at ground level under the sides of the tent. It was obviously a cooking fire from outisde. He took the girl's nude, warm body in his arms and held her close. She was firm and smooth against him, surprisingly womanly. She tried to pull back in the darkness, then came forward with a sigh to nestle against him.

"I was only trying to keep you warm," she whispered.

"I know. Thank you." He paused. "Did they hurt you?"

"No. Some of the men wanted to—take me—but the chief said no, and he had to hit one with the rifle, and ever since we've been here alone. No food, no water, no fire. I don't know what they plan to do. I can understand some of their dialect. They're wandering nomads. Chou hired them to ambush Zhirnov. Did you see Chou?"

"He's dead," Durell said.

"But—did you speak to him at all?"

"He was a good servant of his state," Durell said, "but in the end, he spoke only old heresies."

"The dragon?"

"He tried for it, but Zhirnov was too quick for him. Zhirnov shot him, broke his spine. When that happened, Chou's tribesmen turned their attention to looting the car. Then we came along." He thought of the secret luggage space in the wrecked Ferrari, a space that only he and Nuri Qam knew about, but which someone had opened, someone who must also have known about it. He didn't mention it to the girl in his arms. He said, "It's my bet that Zhirnov got back to the road and bought himself a lift on a passing truck. Maybe he killed the driver. He must be still going south, getting farther and farther ahead of us while we're here. Do you have any idea what time it is, Anya?"

"It turned dark only a couple of hours ago."

"Then I've been out for about four hours?"

"Yes." She paused. "Sam?"

"Ummm?"

"Don't," she whispered.

"I can't help it," he said, aware of the revived heat in him.

"You do not love me, of course."

"We have to keep warm."

"Not this way."

"Why not?"

"You have a woman back home?"

"Home is far away."

"You love her? You are married?"

"No, not married. I can't afford any strings to my life. I won't give the opposition any handle by which they can reach me."

"That is a selfish attitude. If she loves you and wishes to assume the risks of your work, you should still be willing to accept her into your life—"

"You're too serious."

"Love is serious. We Russians—"

"You're no different from others. My work is serious, too. Do you have a man back in Moscow, Anya?"

"Yes," she whispered.

"And Moscow is a long way from here, too."

"Yes."

He touched silent tears on her small face. He heard the footsteps of the guard pacing around the tent. Anya's breath quickened helplessly as they lay entwined in the dark. The guard's boots paused, then went on again, circling the tent. Anya came back to him with a little whispered moan . . .

"Yes, Sam . . . oh, yes . . ."

Later, he searched the tent, feeling his way in the darkness with extreme care to avoid alerting the tribesmen outside. Now and then he heard guttural voices speaking, not too far away. The smell of the cooking fires slowly died away. The night grew colder. The tent was twelve feet in diameter, he judged, supported by four corner poles that kept the tattered covering no more than four feet over their heads. The floor was only the cold, rocky shale, but then in one corner near the pole he found a heap of sheepskins that had been tossed aside. Underneath the skins, to his pleasure and surprise, he found his khaki bush jackets and slacks and boots, and Anya's clothing as well. The pockets were all empty, of course; his papers, money and weapons were gone, grabbed by thieving fingers. Still, he was grateful for the find. He crouched back toward Anya and knelt beside her with her clothing.

"Here. We can stay warm legitimately, now."

She dressed quickly in the darkness, but the gleam of firelight that seeped under the flap of the tent revealed her slim, rounded body as she pulled on her clothes.

"What will they do with us, Sam?" she whispered.

"Nothing, at the moment. I think the camp is all asleep, except for our guard stomping around outside."

"But in the morning?" she asked.

"I don't think they're going to kill us; they would have done so already, if that was their intention. Maybe they have some idea of holding us for ransom. Or—" He paused.

"Or what, Sam?"

"Some of these mountain tribes still go in for slavery. There was a whole people once, related to Hazara tribe, who were enslaved for centuries. Some of that nasty habit probably still survives. There's very little law that can reach into the Hazarajat."

She shuddered. "I'd rather they killed us."

"Not I," Durell said lightly. "We're still alive, and that's the main thing."

"But they beat you so awfully—"

"Yes, I still ache. Don't remind me of it. By the way, Freyda Hauptman-Graz was with Chou, when Chou hired these people to trap Zhirnov. Have you seen anything of her?"

"What I saw, I don't want to remember."

"She's here?" he asked.

"In the next tent. I heard her screaming for what seemed hours." Anya's voice was tight. "They pegged her out in the tent, after stripping her, and I guess every man in the group had her, one after the other." She paused again. "I kept waiting, wanting to die, thinking I would be next. But they didn't come into this tent; I don't know why, except maybe because you were here."

Durell thought about it. Zhirnov had escaped Chou's trap, certainly—the trap that had turned itself on Chou and the German woman; perhaps the bandits knew that Anya was Russian, like Zhirnov, and planned to learn from her what it was that Zhirnov had that was so valuable. The question of Anya would not be pleasant. And it meant that their time was rapidly running out. At any time the mood seized him, the chief of the group could be coming for the girl.

He did not discuss it with Anya. His eyes had adjusted to the darkness in the tent, and he could see her with fair clarity as she sat with her knees under her chin, rocking slightly, her pale face watching him. The faint light from under the tent flap was broken regularly by the shadows of the guard's boots as he circled the tent. There was nothing helpful in their sheepskin prison. Not even a knife to cut their way out, nor a stone he could use as a weapon. His head ached less, and the slow movements he had made as he searched the tent had eased the stiffness of his bruised muscles. He did not think they would be allowed to remain here unmolested until morning.

He knelt beside Anya. "I'm going to try to slip out and explore a bit. Will you be all right now?"

"Don't go away from me," she said. "I'm sorry, I—I'm not myself, you see, so much has happened to confuse me—"

"Still thinking of Zhirnov?"

"Yes. I have been disloyal to him, believing I am right in suspecting that he really works for General Goroschev, in Moscow—the man who imprisoned Colonel Skoll—"

"Cesar Skoll won't stay in jail too long," Durell said. "Not if I know him as I think I do. He'll manage to expose Goroschev's plan to instigate war—and then it will all be over."

"But—but what will happen to me?" Anya asked.

"You can always come to the States," he suggested.

"No, I will not be a defector."

He spoke gently. "It will work out. Stay here. Don't move about to attract the guard's attention. I'll be back in a few minutes."

She said simply, "I am frightened."

18

He moved to the far side of the tent where the flap was up and got down on his stomach and peered out. At first he could see only a dim red glow from the campfire; then he made out the black shapes of other tents nearby. He counted four, with the shapes of tethered camels beyond, against a rise of rock. There were no more than a dozen of the beasts, and since the women usually walked and the camels carried camp equipment, he assumed there were about a dozen fighting men in the group, as well.

He ducked back when the guard's booted feet came around the tent. The man came very close to the low-pitched edge of the tent. Durell looked up at the sky and saw a bright spatter of stars against cold velvet. The tip of the moon gleamed above a jagged ridge of mountains. They could not have traveled far from the ambush site, but their elevation here in these wild hills was high enough to cause the night's biting cold. The other tents were pitched in a rough line at the base of a rock abutment for shelter from the wind. That meant the next tent was the one where Freyda had met her agonies.

The sentry's boots sounded again. Flat on his stomach, Durell waited, then suddenly slid out from under the tent flap, grabbed the man's ankle, yanked hard. There was a muffled sound from the guard, but before his voice lifted in a yell of alarm, Durell had him down with a heavy thud and clapped a hand over his mouth. The man's rifle clattered as it fell. He was wearing Durell's wristwatch. His clothing stank of rancid fat and sweat. The shock of his sudden fall had knocked the breath out of him, and Durell's stiff fingers stabbed for his larynx. The man tried to jerk his way free; he was thickset and strong, but there was no air in his lungs when Durell cut it off. They were locked together for a long minute while the man thrashed under him. Durell watched the eyes change, popping, growing glazed; he stabbed deeper and something suddenly crushed. There was a strong sound from deep inside the sentry's body, a tremor, and then the guard was still.

Durell did not move, waiting and listening. The noise made by the guard's falling rifle had seemed quite loud, but no one came to investigate. The camp was asleep. But it would not be so for long, he thought grimly.

He got to his feet, picked up the rifle. He also retrieved his watch from the dead man's wrist. Erect, he could see that the camp was pitched close to a wall of a narrow pass in the mountains. A stream tumbled down through the rocks a bit below the site. There were only the five tents he had counted. The dung fire was almost out, leaving only a small heap of glowing coals occasionally spitting sparks in the gusty cold wind. No other tribesmen were outside the tents.

The rifle felt reassuring as he moved toward the adjacent tent. In a moment he brushed aside the flap and stepped inside, ducking low under the black hide covering.

"Freyda, don't make a sound," he whispered.

There was a muffled whimpering from the darkness that reeked around him. He closed the tent flap and heard a scraping noise, a quick inhalation of breath; his foot touched a leg and he dropped quickly to his knees.

"Freyda? It's me. Sam Durell."

"Oh, no, *nicht* . . ." The words became garbled German. He smelled blood inside the tent. Even though he was only a foot or two away from the woman, he could not see her. "It is so?" she finally gasped. "It is the Cajun?"

"Keep your voice down."

"But how did you—why should you—?"

"Are you badly hurt?" he whispered.

"Hurt? Ach, yes, I am hurt. A young girl dreams of men, older women dream of men, but these are stinking, filthy animals. Shall I tell you the things they made me do, naked before them, one after the other—"

He clapped a hand over her mouth to quiet her rising hysteria. He was glad he could not see her in the darkness. He said, "Did you know that Chou is dead?"

"So? What do I care for that Chinese? It was all his fault, in any case. If not for my sister in Peking—"

"She's dead, too," he said bluntly.

He felt her body jerk as if he had struck her. But he knew that brutality was necessary. "Listen, Freyda. It came over the Peking radio. Madame Strelsky and the General—both dead in an alleged lover's quarrel. There's no reason to doubt it, do you understand? She will never leave China now. She will be buried there."

"No."

"It's true."

"No! Go away."

A sob caught in her throat. He moved back a little and waited. Freyda was silent for a long time. Her teeth finally began to chatter. He was ready to stifle her if she screamed or raised her voice.

"Freyda?" he whispered.

"What do you want?"

"I need your help."

"From me?" Her laughter was harsh, almost soundless. "You have not seen what I look like now. My face—they used knives. My breasts, my stomach, my feet. I cannot walk. How can I help you?"

"Did you see Zhirnov?"

"Him? Yes."

"Is he here in the camp?"

"Oh, no. That one is like a cat. He got away from Chou and his men."

"You're sure of that?" It was as Durell had suspected.

"With the *verdamnt* dragon, yes." She paused. "And Chou turned on these savages and shouted at them and they rejected his appeal and attacked *us*—we, who paid them in the first place. They are treacherous, inhuman—"

"All right." He silenced her. "I'll come back."

"Do not hurry," she said.

He slipped silently out of the tent. But he chose an unfortunate moment to make his exit. Two men had just come out of the tent beyond the dying fire. Both carried rifles, but they held them loosely, muzzles pointed down. They saw Durell at the same moment he spotted them. He could not stop their shouts of alarm. One of them, bulky in a heavy Army coat, raised his rifle, an automatic Kalashnikov. Durell fired at once, his slug hitting the man in the chest, knocking him backward with his legs in the air as he hit the ground. The second man shouted and ducked back, and Durell ran across the campground, hurtling over the glowing fire, and got back to Anya's tent. The rifle he had taken from the guard back there swung lightly in his hand.

"Come out, Anya! Quickly!"

The girl had trained reflexes. She ducked out into the cold night air at a low crouch that made her a small target. All around the camp, there were shouts and yells as men tumbled from their tents. Durell retreated with Anya out of the dark red glow of the firelight, backing toward the opening of the little ravine. Moonlight showed him black-and-white images of the turmoil among the tents. He fired high over the heads of the confused tribesmen and retreated another dozen paces to the shelter of some boulders. A glance over his shoulder showed him the trail down the mountain from the river road where they had first been ambushed. All around him, the hills were a contorted sea of cruel peaks and jagged valleys. He could only judge his general direction by the position of the moonrise.

"It is hopeless," Anya gasped. "We cannot escape."

The men still shouted and ran from tent to tent in the gloom. The wind made a piping sound, blowing dust up from the ground. Durell lifted the rifle and fired two more shots as several figures started toward them.

"Stay here," he said to Anya. "I'm going back."

She was appalled. "What for? We can run—"

"Freyda needs help. And they have my money—"

Most of the tribesmen had vanished, leaving only the man he had first hit sprawled beyond the campfire. Durell ran in a zigzag course back to the fire. A single shot whipped out of the darkness, seeking him out. He ignored it, reached the fallen man as another shot smashed into the stony ground nearby. The dead man was big, muffled in his Army coat with flaps that spread around him and made him look like a giant, fallen insect. The shadow of the cliffs provided adequate darkness. Durell put down the rifle and rapidly searched the dead man. The tribesman had been a chief, evidently. He found his wallet, passport and .38 handgun almost at once. Luck, he thought. But the luck did not hold. When he arose again, only moments later, two men hurtled at him out of the cold, windy darkness.

His reflexes were still slowed by the beating he had taken when they first captured him. The first man jumped feet first, his boots slamming into Durell's ribs, knocking him over. He rolled, grabbed at a leg, pulled the tribesman down over him before the second man could fire into his exposed body. They rolled over and over toward the glowing embers of the fire, then into the hot coals. The caravan man landed face first into the pit and screamed from the depths of his gut as his face was seared. Durell kept rolling, the coals clinging to the back of his coat; he smelled charred cloth and broiled flesh from his enemy's face. The second man circled, rifle ready, as Durell, on his back, kicked upward and caught him in the groin with the heel of his boot. From the other side of the camp came screams and yells as several camels broke loose and lumbered out into the darkness. The camels were more precious to these people than anything else. With their chief dead, they were close to panic, and their attention was divided between recapturing Durell and the big animals. Durell scrambled up and ran for Freyda's tent.

Someone else was in the dark interior beside the injured woman. He saw the flicker of a knife as the person arose from the prone figure. A hissing spate of dialect came at him and then the knife flashed and he felt the curved point hiss through his sleeve. He grabbed for the other's wrist and twisted, felt a twinge in his battered ribs, and twisted harder. He realized it was a woman, perhaps one of the tribesmen's wives. He swung his fist in a roundhouse blow that knocked the woman off her feet and across the tent. Picking up her knife, he found a match in his jacket and struck it. His fingers shook. One glance in the tiny bomb flare was enough.

Freyda's throat had been cut from ear to ear.

The tribeswoman hissed at him in her mountain dialect that needed no interpreter to make her meaning clear. Durell took the bloody knife with him and ducked out of the low tent, ignoring her. Gunfire sounded up the narrow pass as the men tried to retrieve their stampeding camels. He ignored it, ignored the bodies of the men he had killed by the campfire, and jogged back to where he had left Anya.

A man was with her. It was Howard, from the van.

"Oh, it's you," Howard said calmly. "I came back to see if I could help."

He held a hunting rifle competently, as if he knew how to use it. His young grin made his white teeth flash in the moonlight. "I guess I missed all the excitement."

Durell suddenly felt exhausted. "You okay, Anya?"

"Yes. But Freyda—"

"Forget it." He turned to the young man. "Where is your van?"

"Back on the road, about four miles from here. Most of the way is downhill. Need some help, Mr. Durell?"

"No, I'm all right," Durell said.

"You look funny. They really beat up on you, didn't they? Lucy can fix you up. She studied nursing for a while. And I was a corpsman for a year, in Nam."

"That may come in handy," Durell said.

He took Anya's hand and they started down the narrow pass, moving quickly away from the caravan camp.

19

Southward were the salt lakes of the Gaud-i-Zirreh. To the north was the Khash desert. The road was mostly dirt, paved only in sections where dam construction on the Khash and Helmand Rivers was in progress. The heat was intolerable. The mountains were far behind them, and it was noon of the second day of their tortuous drive south after they left the wrecked Ferrari. Chakhansur shimmered like a mirage ahead, a spot of green oasis in the barren land. Howard and George slept in the back of the van. Lucy and Anya sat up front with Durell. He had allowed Howard to drive for a few hours during the night, then returned to the wheel at dawn. His weariness went bone-deep from the irregular jolting on the rippled dirt roads. Groups of nomads in their black woolen robes, herding camels and goats, passed now and then on the trail. A few construction trucks also occupied the track. They had stopped at midmorning at a small village near the Khash-Rud, where a *hammam,* a small Turkish bath in a government-sponsored inn, was available. There were no facilities for the girls. Later, Lucy prepared a meal for them on the van's propane stove. From the post office next to the *hammam,* Durell had tried to call Sarah Fingal in Meshed. It was impossible to get a connection this time.

In Chakhansur, a place that seemed as remote as the moon, he tried again. Some Americans worked here on another of the dams, but the town was dusty and secretive behind its blank house walls and drooping date palms. The jail stood at one end of a small square, flanked by two mosques with minarets that scratched at the brazen sky. Although the Helmand Lakes were just twenty miles off, there was no relief from the heat. In ancient times, this area had been fertile and prosperous, until the Mongols laid it waste and destroyed the *qanats* that brought water underground from the rivers. Most of the laborers were Hazaras here, a cheerful, hard-working tribe universally scorned and avoided by the rest of the population, for reasons lost in the darkness of the past.

It took only twenty minutes to get through to Sarah Fingal this time, while Howard and George and Lucy wandered about the dusty square and considered the tiled mosques on either side of the government building. The clerk inside was efficient. When Durell heard Sarah's voice above a thin crackling in the phone, he blew out a breath of relief.

"Sarah?"

"Oh, good, Sam. Are you all right?"

"Reasonably. Did you get Washington?"

"I spoke to McFee himself." Sarah's voice was crisp and alert, unlike the dullness that had clouded her mind after learning of Homer's death. "McFee gave me quite a handful for you, and a lot of instructions for me. You haven't gotten the dragon back, have you?"

"No."

"You won't find Professor Berghetti in jail there, either. I've been on the phone, myself, to Hal Oberman in Kabul, early this morning. A man named Andrews, an American, got Berghetti out on forged papers from Kabul at four o'clock this morning."

"Andrews has to be Zhirnov," Durell said.

"And they've both flown the coop. Literally."

Durell said, "The nearest airfield is at Qali-i-Kang. Not far from here."

"But service is irregular," Sarah said. "Zhirnov and Berghetti got a private plane there."

"Heading where?"

"Wait," Sarah said. "McFee said you'd need air transport, too. Jules Eaton was at Karachi. Do you know him?"

"Yes, I know Jules," Durell said.

"Is he a good pilot?"

"One of the best."

"He's bringing a plane for you to Qali-i-Kang. In fact, he should be at the field now, waiting."

"The destination?"

"Well, you asked for some background on the Qam brothers—Dochi and Nuri, your friend who started all this."

"Nuri is not my friend. Not since yesterday."

"Oh? You've got something?"

"I think so," Durell said. "What about the Qams?"

"Art collectors. Millionaires plus. Nuri has a record of three visits to Eastern Europe: Budapest, Warsaw and Sofia. Also two trips to Moscow. No details on any of the trips. But guess why he's a persona non grata in Kabul, and why he's over the border in Meshed these days?"

"He's suspect. Playing hanky-panky with Big Brother to the north. Maybe both Big Brothers."

"How did you get that?" Sarah asked.

"Is Nuri still in that villa in Meshed?"

"I had people check on that, too, Sam. He's gone. Destination is an eighty percent probability, McFee says. Dochi and Nuri share a pretty big estate, pretty posh, on the island of R'as Khasab in the Gulf of Oman. Off the tip of the Iranian coast. Maybe four hundred miles due south of Qali-i-Kang."

"Thank you, Sarah."

"Jules Eaton knows it. You'll have to fly the border illegally, I reckon, but Jules can do it. He knows the territory like a book, from his old geology exploration days. Jules has worked for McFee before. You can trust him, Sam."

"I do."

"Another thing, Sam. General Wellington is out as chief of staff at Sugar Cube, as of last night. McFee got to the Oval Office. Wellington is now posted to Fort Riley, Kansas."

"Two down," Durell said, thinking of Peking.

"What?"

"What's the rest of it?"

"You sound funny, Sam. Strange, I mean."

"I feel strange."

Sarah, enjoying herself now, said, "The last thing, maybe the most important. Our listening post in the Indian Ocean—Station Forty-Four, you know it?—intercepted urgent messages to the USSR helicopter cruiser *Georgi Daghestan* to proceed at full speed to the Gulf of Oman from the ship's post off Bombay. Guess where, Sam?"

"R'as Khasab. Within helicopter range, anyway. To pick up Zhirnov and the dragon."

"You get a gold star, Sam. But you'll have to hurry." Sarah's voice faded on the crackling telephone line, then grew strong again. "You there, Sam?"

"Sarah, you ought to be in the business," he said.

"No, thanks."

At the airfield at Qali-i-Kang, he paid off Howard and George and Lucy. Lucy looked tearful again, but she accepted his money gratefully.

"You won't find work here with Berghetti any more," Durell told them. "He's finished, headed for Moscow, maybe, or Timbuktu. There's enough cash here to get you all home."

"That's for me," Lucy said.

"Me, too," said George.

Howard hesitated. He regarded Durell strangely. "You *are* a spook, aren't you?"

"Whatever you care to think."

"You've got problems, right?"

"Lots of them," Durell said.

"Can I help?"

"I'm surprised," Durell said. It was possible that another gun might be needed. Durell considered the tall, long-haired Vietnam veteran and suddenly nodded. "Yes, come along."

Howard grinned. "Great."

"Do you have a last name?" Durell asked.

"Swiftman. They used to call me Tom Swift. Used to be the name of a series of boys' books, long ago. I've been kidded enough about it, you know?"

Durell nodded and looked across the hot, shimmering airfield. A nondescript Cessna was parked in the slanting shade of one of the hangars. Jules Eaton stood there, waiting.

20

The beer was lukewarm. The room was scorching. At ten o'clock in the evening, the thermometer in the little port town of Bandar-e-Sirri stood at 118°. The humid, fitful wind off the gulf of Oman felt like molten lead in the lungs.

The waterfront hotel room had two windows facing the quai where several Arab dhows were tied up. They were ancient craft, but their lines were swift and graceful, although they were rapidly being replaced by motor fishing boats in the Persian Gulf. The time of romance and exotic shipping presumably had come to an end, replaced by the stink of diesels and the rust of steel plates.

The dhow-master stared at the four of them in the little room. He was a big man, with a dirty white turban and a striped silk shirt whose once gaudy colors had turned gray with sweat. He wore new Keds sneakers. In the waterfront café outside were Indians and Arabs, blacks from Africa, a few European and American engineers involved in the new refinery whose stacks made bloody flames against the night sky. The dhow-master settled his gaze on Durell.

"All of you?" he asked.

"Yes."

"Not the woman."

"Yes."

"I do not take women aboard my vessel."

Durell looked at Anya. "Do you want to go?"

"Yes, Sam."

He looked at the dhow-master. "She wants to go." He counted out more money. "Is that enough to overcome your superstitions?"

"I do not like it."

"Nobody asked you to like it. Just take us out to R'as Khasab. It's not far. No more than an hour. Then you can come back here so much richer."

"There are patrol boats," the man said.

"You can avoid them."

"It is a private island."

"Not any more. Take it or leave it."

The dhow-master scooped up the money and folded it, head down, eyes on it, his rough hands loving the touch of currency. "I will need more for the crew."

"No crew. Just you and your pilot."

"It is not enough to handle the vessel—"

Durell said, "To hell with you, then."

The man licked his lips. "Well, I will try."

They all got up and followed him out to the quai.

Jules Eaton said, "It's a good thing they laid a lot of bread on me in Karachi. Taxpayers' money. You're free enough with it, Cajun."

Durell said, "I have influence with McFee."

"Who is the kid?"

"They call him Tom Swift."

"Who is he? A freak?"

"He looks good enough for an extra hand."

"He shouldn't be in this," Jules said. "He's not in the business. Does he know he might be killed?"

Howard said, "I'm here of my own free will."

"All right, kid. Get your head blown off. Just stay out of my way."

Jules was squat and square, a cube of a man who looked as if he were built entirely out of slabs and planes. His thick black hair and heavy brows made him look more Greek than American. He ran errands for K Section as a sideline to his business in Karachi, whatever that was these days. Jules had taken them across the border, flying low over the lakes and then cutting through the passes of the Mokran, the mountain range south of the salt desert of the Dasht-i-Lut. If any Baluchi nomads in the Mokran noted the plane, no one had reported it. Jules knew how to swing west and south of the radar towers at Zahidan, and then he headed the old Cessna on a course across the Baluchi *ostan* toward the Gulf of Oman coast. They landed on a makeshift strip usually reserved for the refinery people on the outskirts of Bandar-i-Sirri. The landing was made by moonlight. An hour later, the dawn came up in a red haze of furnace heat and the naked hills that separated the coastal plain from the inner desert began to cook in the shimmering haze. The local people shuffled about their daily work, selling pottery and goats, basketwork and donkeys. The women wore bright robes and embroidered baggy pants. The men spent their time sleeping.

They arrived, they found the room, and then nothing happened. The timing was bad, but it couldn't be helped. They had had to fly across the border by night, and it would be foolish to sail for R'as Khasab in broad daylight. They made arrangements for the dhow and waited for darkness to fall. The end of the day did not mean the end of the heat.

While Jules and Howard were on the waterfront, Durell found himself alone in the room with Anya.

She had been silent ever since Jules picked them up at Qala-i-Kang. Now she sat on the edge of the bed, her back bowed, her hands covering her face. Now and then a shudder went through her, and Durell turned from examining the weapons bag Jules Eaton had brought with them in the plane.

"What is it, Annie?"

"Nothing. I am tired, I suppose. It is so warm. I think how futile this all is. We risk our lives and leave death in our paths, and all the time in your country and mine, the whole plot is countered by others, and the dragon becomes unimportant. Except to Moscow, which does not seem to know yet what is happening. Why do you and I go on now?"

"It's a personal matter," Durell said.

"I do not understand."

"A harmless little man named Homer Fingal was betrayed and cruelly murdered. It's something I have to finish up before I go home."

"Home?" Anya picked listlessly at the word. "I will have no home when this is over. I think they will have shot Colonel Skoll by now, and there will be no one to speak for me. I shall be listed as a traitor—at best, as unreliable."

Deep violet smudged her eyes, and her face was pale and shining in the dingy little room. All at once she began to shudder again, shaking her whole body; she hugged herself and her teeth chattered. Durell touched her forehead. It was burning.

"You have a fever," he said gently. "It would be best if you got into bed for a time."

He helped her to undress, surprised again by the ripe contours of her body. The shivering made her cling helplessly to Durell.

"I am still cold."

He found a cloth and used the tap in the room to wet it with tepid water and applied the cloth to her face and body, bathing her gently. Her dark hair fell in tangled skeins over her face. He did not think she was aware of her nakedness.

"I'm so c-cold."

"Hush, Anya."

"Am I sick? Hold me, Sam."

"Yes."

"Tighter, Sam."

"Yes."

After a time she slept. Durell slid out of the bed and sat on the single chair at the window, watching the waterfront. Nothing happened out there. He went back to checking the guns in the waterproof bags Jules Eaton had brought. Two hours later, when Jules and Howard returned, Anya was up, her fever gone. She said nothing as she put on her clothes again. Perhaps, Durell thought, she did not remember anything.

The dhow lifted and fell on the oily waters of the Gulf of Oman. From the quiet murmuring of the diesel, Durell guessed that the below-decks power was unusual, perhaps used for smuggling runs across to the Trucial States of Arabia. The lights of Bandar-i-Sirri were only a dim glow on the horizon, marked by the flares of burning gas towers at the new refineries. They had passed three islands, and now the burly dhow-master turned the wheel a few points to port. It seemed just as hot here on the water as on land. There was no moon, but the stars had a tropical glitter that showed Durell the dark loom of a mile-long island over the bow. The pilot called out something from the bow and the dhow-master turned the wheel another few notches to the left.

"R'as Khasab," he murmured. "You say you do not want to run in to the cove? At the dock?"

"No," Durell said.

"There is a long sandpit, a shallow, to the south. One could wade ashore from there." The man made a contemptuous spitting sound as Howard came aft. "Unless the boy with the girl's hair is afraid of the sharks."

Howard's face tightened. Jules Eaton looked up from where he had been securing the waterproof bags. Anya checked Howard with a quick hand on his arm.

The dhow-master grinned. "Yes, there are many sharks in these waters. Everyone knows that. Are you afraid of them, dear girl?"

From up forward came the pilot's grunt of laughter. The pilot was as big as the dhow's captain. In another century, these two would have qualified as murderous pirates, and their instincts were still alive today. There came a snicking sound as the pilot came aft with a knife in his hand.

"Perhaps we should cut open his pants and see what he truly has there, eh? A young man with such long hair—"

"Leave him alone," Jules said quietly.

Howard said, "I can take care of myself."

The pilot slid in front of Howard, feinting with the knife. Howard did not withdraw. There came a flash of movement, the sudden thrust of a kick, and Howard was poised horizontally in the air as his foot caught the knife and sent it spinning from the pilot's grip, over the rail and into the water with a splash. The pilot shouted with surprise and rushed at the young man, and Howard spun quickly and used his feet again, thudding against the Arab's chest. The dhow captain started to leave the wheel, and Durell checked him. The pilot hit the deck with a thump, scrambled up and rushed at Howard with a bellow of rage. Howard hit him a third time and the man's eyes crossed and he staggered back, hit the rail, and followed his knife into the water with a mighty splash.

Howard drew a deep breath. "Let *him* see if he is afraid of sharks."

The dhow-master twisted away to throw a line to his pilot. "Ali?"

Jules moved casually beside Howard. "Help him out of the water, kid. We don't want him to drown—yet."

Five minutes later, the subdued pilot, dripping and scowling imprecations, was back at his post.

The water was like soup, waist-deep, and Howard and Jules carried the weapons bags on their shoulders as they waded toward the dark, flat shore at the southern tip of R'as Khasab. A row of palms fringed against the starlit sky guided them to the beach. The dhow's motor suddenly throbbed as the vessel turned away. Durell watched it head for the mainland, then helped Jules distribute the weapons. There were two automatic rifles, knocked down and needing assemblage, which they did quickly in the darkness; and two handguns; two thermite bombs; and four grenades. Durell took one of the rifles, Jules Eaton the other.

Howard said, "Give me a couple of the grenades and a pistol. I used 'em in Nam for a full year."

"Fine, kid," said Jules.

"And don't call me kid."

"Fine," Jules said.

They had glimpsed the villa at the opposite end of the island, a full mile away. It was out of sight from where they waded ashore. The beach sand was soft and yielding; it made their progress labored. Now and then there were ridges of driftwood that forced them to detour inland, through the palm trees. The gloom within the groves felt oppressive. No one else seemed to inhabit the island. There was a tumbledown group of shanties halfway up the island, at a small cove, but the fishermen there had long ago been dispossessed. Jules and Howard rapidly scouted the huts and came back signalling the way was clear. In another fifteen minutes, they came upon the first guard, sleeping with his back against a date palm that grew at the edge of the beach.

Jules took the man expertly, holding his gun at his throat, waking him up with a quick, painful prod. The man yelped softly, tried to reach for his gun, and froze as he realized he was about to get his head blown off. He made a gurgling sound of fear.

They surrounded the squirming man. "How many other guards are there?" Durell asked.

"Two only, sir, please—"

"You lie."

"Four, then. No more than four. I swear by Allah—"

"And Nuri Qam?"

"The master is in the house."

"When did he arrive?"

"Yesterday."

"And his guest?"

"The younger man? Yesterday, too."

"Both are still here?"

"Yes, sir. Yes, sir."

"Any other visitors?"

"No, none. But they are waiting—"

"For what?"

"I do not know, sir. It is not my business. I am only one of the guardians of the property, sir. Mr. Qam likes privacy here. We have good employment on R'as Khasab.

All through the year, we are here, we take good care of the property. Mr. Qam is very generous for an Afghani—"

"What are they waiting for?"

"I do not know."

Jules jabbed his throat with the gun. "Don't lie again. When do the next visitors arrive?"

"I am only a servant, sir, but I think—they have not unpacked their luggage, and the guest, Mr. Andrews, he always listens to Mr. Qam's radio. A helicopter, I think. Yes, that's it. They wait for a helicopter."

"Tonight?"

"Yes, most certainly tonight."

"Fine," Durell said.

Jules reversed his gun and slammed it at the man's head. The guard's eyes rolled up and he slumped away. Anya tore a strip of cloth from her shirttail and made a gag, while Howard swiftly bound the man with some line he carried. They went on, following a path across a small rocky rise, and came in sight of Nuri Qam's villa.

It was built in the Eastern style, with four high walls forming a quadrangle that surrounded a tiled inner court. Watered gardens, oleander shrubs, pistachio trees and palms made the place an oasis of bright blossoms. Bougainvillea spilled over some of the inner balconies. The outer wall was about fifteen feet high, surrounding the enclave except for an area of the seawall, where a white motor yacht was moored to a small stone quai. Lights shone through tall, narrow windows on one side of the inner quadrangle.

Durell halted his companions at the far side of brushy knoll. He studied the high dark walls, the single wooden gate with its Moorish arch on this side, a narrow path that angled down from the landward side to a patch of sand along the water, where a striped canopy was stretched beside a swimming pool built into the rock ledge jutting from the beach.

"There," he whispered. "Two of them. Near the gate."

"I don't see them."

"Guards. Smoking."

"Right. No way to get at them without being seen."

"Try it from the pool side. Quietly," Durell took a silencer from his jacket and screwed it into the muzzle of his rifle. "I'll cover you from here, and be there with you."

They were a team of deadly predators now, closing in on the villa. The two guards were unsuspecting. One of them laughed, dragging at his cigarette. It made a brief red glow against the dark shadows at the gate. Jules and Howard were off without a sound. Durell and the girl waited. He counted off twenty seconds, then suddenly saw Jules streaking up from the canopied terrace at the swimming pool.

"Let's go, Annie."

The guard with the cigarette saw Jules just before the chunky man hit him. The second guard lifted his gun and Durell squeezed the trigger and his rifle made a flat, muffled sound. The guard crashed his head against the wall just as Howard hit him below the knees. Durell and Anya ran down the short slope to join the others in the dark shelter of the wall. The guards were unconscious, the one Durell had shot bleeding from the thigh. Jules Eaton used his coil of line to truss them up and glowered down at them.

"Keys," Durell said. "To the gate."

Howard knelt and searched. "No keys."

"Listen," Jules said.

A man called querulously from beyond the high wall. They froze in the dark gateway. The voice called again, then was silent. Durell said, "It's all right. Give me a lift, Jules."

The pilot cupped his hands, Durell stepped up into them, and leaped for the top of the wall. He didn't dare miss. The sound of his fall would arouse sure suspicion within, this time. His fingers clawed for the rough top, slipped, caught. He dangled there, aware of the others watching and holding their breaths. Then he heaved upward, threw his left arm across the wall, felt grateful it wasn't topped with broken glass, and at last scrambled to the top, where he lay flat, surveying the garden and the lighted windows of the villa.

A rope snaked up to him, tossed by Jules. He made it fast while Howard walked up the wall like a mountain climber. Anya came next. Jules waited until Anya and Howard had dropped to the soft grass and oleanders inside before he followed.

"Mahmoud?"

It was the same voice that had queried softly in the darkness before. Durell had no idea how many other men were inside the villa. Servants, of course. Nuri Qam would never travel without a cook or two, a body servant, perhaps a secretary. They would be of no account. Zhirnov was the one to watch for. He tried to see through the lighted windows of the villa, but he could not identify the flickering shadows inside.

Quietly, they moved around to the seaward side of the villa, where the motor yacht was moored. A wide sweep of grass sloped down to the stone bulkheads. Durell's boot touched something sticking up from the grass, and for an instant he felt chilled, aware of the chances of an alarm trigger. Then he saw it was a flare, one of several thrust into the turf to form a landing square to guide in a helicopter. He wondered how much time they had. For a moment his nerves played tricks on him and he imagined he heard the deep pulsing of a chopper's blades coming from the Soviet cruiser. But the velvet night sky was empty. Soon enough, he thought grimly.

All at once he saw the dhow.

It should have been halfway to the mainland by now. Instead, it appeared beyond a small point about half a mile from the villa, on the far side of the island.

He knew what it meant. The sullen dhow-master and his pilot, smarting and vengeful, had been here at the villa, talking to those within.

And at that moment, the roof fell in.

The peaceful quiet suddenly exploded with fire and noise. An automatic gun opened fire from an upper balcony of the villa. Durell threw himself flat, dragging

Anya down to the terrace floor with him. Bullets smashed and chipped at the tiles and sent sprays of water from the hexagonal fountain nearby. He heard a strange sound from young Howard, a growling yell from Jules Eaton. He wriggled forward with Anya to the shelter of the fountain. When he turned his head, he saw Howard still upright, throwing one of his grenades. It burst with a tremendous blast up there on the gallery, and Durell got up and ran forward under the shelter of the balcony. Anya was close beside him. There came a stuttering fire from Jules, then more firing came from the left, slapping and crackling along the fine tilework of the wall. A handful of chips stung the side of his face.

"Up the steps, Annie."

She was right with him, her face pale, holding her handgun and pulling the pin of one of her grenades. She lobbed it forward at the stairs and they threw themselves flat, then raced for the smoking steps and went up. Durell heard Jules's gun hammering at the upper balconies and then he was at the top, yelling for Jules to hold it. A figure suddenly loomed before him, gun held at the hip. Durell fired, the man skittered backward, went over the balcony rail with a long, surprised wail.

There is a technique to such a raid, a rule that says never to pause, to keep going against any odds, lobbing grenades, firing murderously into any room, never stopping it. Anya knew the rule, too. They wreaked devastation as they ran along the balcony, throwing the thermite bombs, keeping their guns hammering. Similar sounds came from the opposite end of the balcony, and he knew Jules was doing the same work. Just once, he turned to look down at the seafront terrace. A figure lay there, sprawled on its face, near the man he had shot down from the balcony.

There came a pleading shriek of terror from beyond arches of the gallery. The room there was dark.

"Hold it, Anya."

He checked the lob of her grenade. Her face was taut.

"Nuri?" he called.

"Ah, Sam, *Sam!*"

"Come out here."

"No. No."

"Where is Zhirnov?"

"Gone."

"Where?"

"To the tower."

"With the dragon?"

"He has the dragon, yes."

"Come out here," Durell said again.

"No."

The stink of explosions drifted in the air. He signalled Anya to stay back, then jumped across the doorway to the other side. An automatic opened up as he crossed over, spraying wild bullets at him. He flattened against the wall, holding his gun high and ready. Scuttling noises came from within. He took one of the thermite bombs and lobbed it inside. There came a flash and bursting sound and flames roared in the room. There was a scream and another burst of gunfire, and then Durell dived inside. In the lurid light of burning chemicals, he saw Nuri Qam dart through an inner doorway. He did not wait for Anya this time. There was shouting, and a man's voice responded. A figure suddenly darted in the inner doorway and Durell fired a short burst. The man stumbled aside. Durell jumped over him. He was in a long corridor that paralleled the dock area below. Through the row of delicate pillars and arches, he could see the boat at its mooring and the tall spire of a minaret tower at the opposite end of the quadrangle. Someone was running away from him, down the gallery.

"Nuri!"

Nuri Qam did not stop.

Durell fired once at the man's fleeing heels. Nuri skidded on the tiles, fell forward with a thump, his stout body bouncing. Durell ran cautiously after him. Nuri tried to rise, but he was hampered by the sling in which his shoulder was bound. Flames crackled behind Durell. Nuri Qam's round face quaked as he looked into the muzzle of Durell's gun.

"It's over, Nuri."

"No, no."

"You'll never make it. You didn't have time to alert your other guards, did you? The dhow-master tipped you off, right? You're waiting for the chopper from the Soviet ship. You and Zhirnov—you're taking off for Moscow. You threw in with the Russians long ago, I figure. They own you, Nuri."

"My wife—my favorite wife—she is in Moscow now—"

"A prisoner?"

"On technical charges. They only wanted me to do small things for them, in Kabul. I was afraid. I had to do it. In any case—"

"In any case, your sympathies were with the USSR all along. That's why you're in political trouble back home."

"Yes, but—" Nuri Qam tried to struggle to his feet. Durell pushed him down with the muzzle of his gun, and said, "Peking isn't taking the bait. Washington is out of it, too. Moscow is beating a dead horse. Nobody cares who has the dragon now."

"I—I care," Nuri Qam gasped. "Please—"

Gunfire burst from the other end of the villa, where Jules worked his way from room to room. Now and then he heard the roar of a grenade as Anya did the same, behind him. But everything seemed to have stopped at this place, in this time. Durell looked down at the frightened figure of his former classmate. So many years ago, he thought. So much was different now. He saw Nuri Qam plead with his eyes, and he went grim.

"If you had the dragon, Nuri, why did you call me into it in the first place?"

Nuri Qam gasped. "But I didn't—I didn't have the dragon then. Berghetti had hidden it; he took it with him when he escaped from protective custody. He's dead now, I think. I believed—I thought you were the only man who could get the dragon back for me. That was before Zhirnov contacted me. Before I caught up with Berghetti and got the dragon for myself and went to Meshed. It was too late to ask Washington to call you back. It would have looked odd. Please, Sam, for old time's sake—we were friends once?"

"You tried to kill me. You killed Homer Fingal."

"Zhirnov's man, Kokin, did that!"

"All the same. You worked together. You used me."

Qam said, puzzled, "How are you so sure—"

"The Ferrari," Durell explained. "Zhirnov wrecked it and we found it. The secret compartment behind the luggage space had been opened. Only you could have told Zhirnov how to open it. That's when I knew you and Zhirnov were together."

"Yes. Yes, I see. But—"

"You're going back to Kabul, Nuri."

"No, they will hang me!" Qam shouted. Ignoring Durell's gun, he lurched to his feet, hugging his wounded arm. His eyes shone with irrational terror. He had a Luger in his hand, suddenly. As he swung it to fire at Durell, there came a single, careful shot from the gallery. Nuri spun around, clutching at his chest. His eyes popped with astonishment, he made a strangling sound, and his fat legs turned to rubber as he collapsed to the gallery floor. His gun clattered and slid over the edge to the terrace below.

Durell saw Anya run toward him in the blinding glare of fire behind her.

At the same time, he heard the beat and thud of a helicopter's rotors in the black sky above.

21

"Jules?"

The pilot appeared out of the gloom. Jules Eaton scarcely glanced at Nuri Qam's dead body.

"Zhirnov is up in the tower," Durell said.

"Yo."

"Have you seen Howard?"

"No. How do we get up there?"

"Good question."

A brilliant shaft of light suddenly poured down from the black sky. The chopper up there was a big one, a new Russian KV-20 model. The sound of its descent grew louder as it lowered to a landing on the seafront terrace. Its searchlights played back and forth on the burning villa. The thermite bombs were doing their work. Apparently the flames confused the Russian pilot. He checked his descent and the helicopter swung out to sea in a wide circle for another approach. Durell studied the tower. It was hexagonal-sided, all blue and gold tiles, with a bulbous spire on the top and a small iron-railed walk just below the bulb. He saw something move up there. A man, clutching something to his chest. It would be Zhirnov, he thought, with the dragon box. In a sense, it no longer mattered. Peking would not take the bait. There would be no rumbles of war, no blistering diplomatic notes, no preemptive strikes from either side of the Siberian border. But Zhirnov did not know that. And Durell suddenly held Sarah Fingal's thin, mournful face in his mind, and thought of Homer's ugly death in the desert. sert.

Jules said, "There's one door at the base of the tower. There. Probably a spiral stairway up to the gallery at the top. Like shooting ducks in a rain barrel, Cajun. No way to get up there against him."

The chopper came back from over the calm, oily sea. Its searchlight flickered and probed, found the tower, bathed its blue projectilelike height in a dazzling glow. Now Durell could see the door at the top, a wooden panel that opened onto the gallery that went around the six-sided tower. Nobody was in sight there now. The underbelly of the chopper hovered directly over the tower. Suddenly a small hatch opened and a weighted ladder tumbled downward. It swung wide, swung back, hit the tower with a tangled thump, and was withdrawn a bit while the pilot steadied his aircraft.

"He's good," Jules Eaton murmured.

"I must get up there," Anya said.

"No way," Jules told her. "By the time he stops covering the inside steps to get out on the balcony, there wouldn't be a chance for us to get up. He's going to make it."

"No," Anya said bitterly. "He must not."

She raised her gun and aimed it at the high doorway.

Durell said, "Fire a couple of rounds, Anya, so he'll know we're covering his exit up there."

She did as she was told. They could see the bullets smashing into the small paneled door high above. The door started to open inward and Zhirnov appeared, holding the dragon box. Another shot drove Zhirnov inside again.

"Keep it up," Durell ordered.

He turned and ran for the base of the tower. One of the chopper's spotlights caught him, but there was no fire from the aircraft. In a matter of seconds, he was at the lower door to the tower. The ladder from the chopper

swung high above, at the level of the upper gallery fifty
feet in the air. Anya fired again, and then Jules Eaton's
heavier rifle took over. Durell opened the lower door.
Dim light came down the interior of the hexagonal tower
from the chopper's spotlights. Something stirred up there.
A shot bellowed savagely in the narrow interior. The bullet spattered against the stone wall. Durell caught the iron
rail of the inner steps and ran upward, gun raised, his
back scraping against the rough stone.

"Zhirnov!"

A second shot crashed, echoed deafeningly.

"Give it up, Zhirnov! You can't get out!"

He slid up two more steps. Jules Eaton had been right.
He was a duck in a rain barrel. Over the thudding of his
pulse in his ears, he heard the rythmic beat of the chopper's blades. A loudspeaker called something in Russian.
The words were like those of a giant descending from the
sky. Durell heard the slap of the craft's ladder against the
outer wall. Zhirnov had left the upper door open a crack,
and the floodlight outside bathed his face momentarily.
Durell fired and instantly ran up half a dozen more steps.
Zhirnov's gun stuttered, seeking him out. Then the man
threw open the outer door and tried to lunge out and grab
the swinging ladder lowered from above.

There came the sound of one carefully aimed shot.

It was Anya's gun.

Durell went up the inner stairs in a swift, desperate
rush. Zhirnov crashed back through the doorway and
slumped to the platform floor up there. Durell went up
the rest of the steps two and three at a time, and slammed
the muzzle of his gun into Zhirnov's throat.

There was no need to pull the trigger.

Anya had shot him neatly through the heart.

The chopper did not go away. Apparently, the pilot
could not figure out what was happening. The persistent
beat of its blades was a drumbeat in the black sky. Durell
picked up the ornate box that had fallen from Zhirnov's
grip and saw it had been damaged at one corner and the
lid sprung up.

Inside was the dragon.

Small and serene, its jade sides glowing with inner fire as the chopper's spotlight poured through the open door, the beast held the pearl that represented the soul of the moon still secure between its golden teeth. The ruby eyes held secrets no man would know. The golden egg in its belly felt soft and warm under Durell's fingers.

It was not worth the price.

He stepped carefully out on the little balcony. He meant to wave the helicopter away, but it had already swung aside to hover over the lawn that led down to the little dock. From this height, he could see the quadrangle clearly. Someone ran across the grass, followed by the spotlight and the ladder. It was Anya. She signalled in an obviously predetermined way and the Russian pilot followed her. The ladder dropped lower and she grabbed for the rungs, whipped her legs around it for a secure grip, and was promptly hoisted upward. The roar of the helicopter's engines increased suddenly and the craft tilted, swung away from the island and beat its way out over the dark waters of the Gulf of Oman. The last Durell saw of it, the girl was still climbing up toward the hatch.

Jules Eaton's voice echoed up the tower.

"Cajun?"

"I'm all right," said Durell.

"You've got it?"

"I've got it."

"What in hell made the girl do that?"

Durell did not have to think about it. "She wanted to go home," he said.

"Well, that boy Howard won't be going home. He's dead. They got him in the first ambush fire."

"I know," Durell said quietly.

"Amateurs," Jules Eaton muttered.

"He only wanted to help."

Jules waited at the bottom of the tower stairs. His square face was impersonal. The sound of the helicopter faded away to the south. The island was quiet, except for the crackling of the flames as the villa burned.

Jules shrugged heavy, slablike shoulders. He did not ask to examine the dragon. He did not care about it.

"We can take Nuri Qam's power boat back to the mainland," he said. "And use the plane to get to Tehran. The sooner you're back on a flight to the States, Cajun, the better. I'll square the authorities if there are any questions. Right now, we'd better make tracks like a coon with a fire up its tail."

"Yes," Durell said.

He walked toward the dock with Jules Eaton, holding the dragon gently in both hands.

22

It was raining in Washington. Fog covered the Potomac Basin. At nine o'clock in the morning, Durell had a surprise visitor at his apartment. He was making a pot of Louisiana coffee, a rasher of bacon and three eggs, with juice, for breakfast. His apartment overlooked the park, with its fallen leaves and dripping brown tree branches. Mist moved along the park paths. He had checked the cars in the street below, and everything seemed normal. Checking was part of his regular routine. His books needed dusting, and the tomes of law from his graduate school days, aging on his shelves, needed a thorough cleaning. His desk was tidy, his leather armchair by the good reading lamp welcomed him. When the doorbell rang from the lobby below, he waited. When it rang again, three short times, he pressed the buzzer and then went back to his breakfast.

His visitor was General Dickinson McFee, boss of K Section. The small gray man looked unhappy to be away from his aerie on the top floor of No. 20 Annapolis Street. He shook water from his knobby blackthorn walking stick as Durell helped him out of his raincoat.

"Good morning, Samuel. I've brought you some of our accumulated mail."

"Thank you, sir."

"And your debriefing report."

"Yes, sir?"

"Some matters of commission—and omission."

"Yes, sir. Have you had breakfast, General?"

"Samuel, I am in no mood to eat."

"Then excuse me, sir. I'm very hungry."

"Yes, you've been sleeping for twenty-four hours."

"Yes, sir. I needed it."

Durell took the letters and dropped them on his desk and went into the small kitchen, dried the bacon on paper towels, slipped his scrambled eggs from the iron skillet, and poured a mug of the chicory-flavored coffee, then set everything on a wooden Swedish tray and carried it to his desk. McFee sat in the red leather armchair, his blackthorn stick held upright between his knees.

"Commission and omission," McFee repeated. Rain rattled against the windows. "Open your mail, Samuel."

"Why? Have you read it already?"

"I took the liberty, yes."

Durell surveyed the two envelopes. The seal on the flaps seemed unbroken. "Nice work. Abe Steelman's?"

"I opened them myself. Aren't you curious?"

Durell bit into his toast, forked some bacon and eggs, chewed thoughtfully, his blue eyes dark with thought. Not until he had had some of his home-brewed coffee did he open the envelopes. The first letter bore a Swedish stamp and was postmarked from Stockholm. It was in the peculiar crabbed hand of a European, in English, and it read:

Dear Sam—
 We know your headquarters address, of course. This is just a brief word to let you know I returned safely. Moscow had a different atmosphere when I arrived. There have been no problems and few questions. My mission failed, but no one is interested any longer. It was all for nothing—which is for the best.
 Is the dragon beautiful?

Annie.

McFee was watching him with cool gray eyes.

"Your KGB collaborator?"

"Yes, sir, if you want to put it that way."

"Precisely, Samuel. Open the other letter."

"I'm glad she's safe."

"To be sure."

Durell opened the second envelope. It bore two Syrian stamps and was postmarked—and censored—from Damascus. Airmail, he noted. This letter, too, was written in a cramped hand.

My dear Cajun—

Once again I owe you thanks. Anya told me kindly of your activities. Quite admirable. I am free again and on duty. I wish I could have been there. I might have been helpful. But now I must accept reluctantly the burden of another debt to you.

What will you do with P'an Ku's old companion?
                                                Cesar Skoll.

Durell pushed the letters aside and finished his breakfast. McFee waited. Durell had no intention of making the first remark. A car passed by on the wet street below, tires whining. He looked at the logs laid in his fireplace across the room. It would be pleasant to spend the evening with a fire going.

McFee lifted his blackthorn stick and tapped the top of the desk with it. "Well, Samuel?"

"Don't point that thing at me, sir. It makes me nervous. I know how the lab boys loaded that stick."

"Omission, Samuel."

Durell said mildly, "The dragon, you mean?"

"Its final disposition is not mentioned in your reports, or in the addenda added to it, or in the debriefing we had to give Sarah Fingal and Jules Eaton."

"I see. You want to know where it is?"

"I expect you to tell me," McFee said.

"Right. Look behind you."

McFee turned his head to look into the open bedroom door. Peeping around the base of the door was the dragon's head, gold teeth gleaming, the large pearl clenched carefully between the fangs upon the ruby tongue. It seemed to be laughing as it tasted the soul of the moon.

"A *doorstop?*"

"Yes, sir," Durell said.

"Samuel, you can't—"

"What would you like me to do with it, sir?"

"Samuel, in any art market, it is worth over five million dollars."

"And it would earn a lot of publicity," Durell pointed out. "We're not supposed to have it."

McFee frowned. "You'll have to turn it in."

"Officially? Perhaps to the National Art Gallery?"

"Samuel, don't be flippant with me."

"I'm open to suggestions then," Durell said. "Think about it."

"You can't just keep it here!"

"No, sir."

"Some way must be devised to get it back to the Afghani authorities," McFee said.

Durell said, "There's a diplomatic reception at the Afghanistan Embassy next week. Perhaps in the form of a little gift, made anonymously—"

"Yes, perhaps. I'll have to consider it."

"On the other hand, it might then never reach Kabul," Durell pointed out.

McFee raised his brows again. He was not normally so expressive. He turned his head again and stared at the dragon on the floor, just beyond the doorway.

"I'll have that cup of coffee with you, Samuel."

"With a little brandy, perhaps?"

"Very good. I'd like that."

"I thought you might," Durell said.